THE BEAUTIFUL CHILDREN

Also by Michael Kenyon

Fiction

Kleinberg (Oolichan Books, 1991)
Pinocchio's Wife (Oberon, 1992)
Durable Tumblers (Oolichan Books, 1996)
The Biggest Animals (Thistledown Press, 2006)

Poetry

Rack of Lamb (Brick Books, 1991)
The Sutler (Brick Books, 2005)

THE BEAUTIFUL CHILDREN

MICHAEL KENYON

thistledown press

Thistledown Press Ltd.
633 Main Street
Saskatoon, Saskatchewan, S7H oJ8
www.thistledownpress.com

Library and Archives Canada Cataloguing in Publication

Kenyon, Michael, 1953 –
The beautiful children / Michael Kenyon.

ISBN 978-1-897235-47-8

I. Title.

PS8571.E67 B43 2009   C813'.54   C2009-900754-1

Cover photograph: Rosanne Olson/Getty Images
Cover and book design by Jackie Forrie
Printed and bound in Canada

10 9 8 7 6 5 4 3 2 1

Thistledown Press gratefully acknowledges the financial assistance of
the Canada Council for the Arts, the Saskatchewan Arts Board, and the
Government of Canada through the Book Publishing Industry Development
Program for its publishing program.

 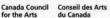

ACKNOWLEDGEMENTS

A portion of the novel appeared in *Prism international* and was subsequently anthologised in *New Canadian Gothic* (Eric Henderson and Madeline Sonik, editors; Turnstone, 1998).

Thanks to the Banff Centre for the Arts and to Robert Kroetsch and Audrey Thomas.

I would like to bless Seán Virgo for being such an uncanny and warmhearted ally during my last long trek with these characters.

All love and thanks to Lorraine, my wife.

*For Tom Kenyon, Muriel Chadwick
and Julia Kenyon*

CONTENTS

All the birds, all the love.
— Dennis Potter

He hath lost his fellows
And strays about to find 'em.
— William Shakespeare

Note

I had been living under the church for
a couple of years, writing down as much
of my life as I could remember, when
I first heard the voices of these children
calling out of the habit of the land.
Mira and the ancestors grew silent
and for a long time the children were guides.
Now they are beginning to fade I wish
to make a gesture, feel their eyes on me
one last time, and entrust them to your care.

BREACH

BREACH BREACH

THE FIRST TIME I GOT UP was evening and I went to the window and looked out and saw a hole, the moist sides glistening. Under misty lights gardeners drove a forklift into the hospital courtyard and unloaded a large tree, roots wrapped in burlap. They seemed concerned about what they were doing yet helpless. As the sky grew dark stars gathered around them. And although I was the sole witness, leaning forward, taking it all in, I had the feeling this was happening for someone else. A person who'd fallen backward into a hole. A man falling while behind him an old woman and an old man slowly danced. I looked away at the white wall of the hospital ward. When I returned my attention to the window what remained was the empty garden, the tree in full bud. A light rain started to spot the glass. I heard a loud crack, as of bone on stone.

The nurse pushed forward a small boy. The doctor leaned over me and said, Don't try to remember, don't struggle, let things happen. The boy said nothing; his black eyes stared. The doctor crept backward and crouched at his side: Try the glove, he said. Show him your glove. The boy came forward and held out the glove. I reached to touch his white fingers. I sat there in bed, in the hospital, with this boy, and sniffed the leather glove until he smiled. When he vanished, I started to breathe, then put my fingers into the glove and cupped my head.

"What did he say?" said the doctor.

"Sapporo," said the nurse. "I think he said Sapporo."

"Isn't that a kind of beer?" said the doctor. "Sapporo. Is that your name?"

I sat on the edge of the bed, looking at my toes, looking down at my feet, my toes, and around me were bodies in other beds. Everything seemed calm, yet beneath the orderliness of white sheets and smiling nurses something was going on a long way away, a long time ago. The window, framed by ivy leaves, overlooked a courtyard where gardeners came and went. My toes wiggled in steady buzzing light and a smell of ointment.

On fine days I walk in the courtyard where thin patients tow machines along narrow paths. Birds sing and sometimes it rains. I don't know who I am. The ward is full of devices that whirr and beep, beds and therapy tables, gurneys and stretchers, washbasins and toilets and baths on wheels, silver handles everywhere. If the doctors and nurses have lives and purposes beyond the hospital walls, I will never learn them. Fear chokes the place. There must be a war going on outside and all the occupants have secrets and know more than I know.

The man falls and falls and blood trickles over his stone pillow; the two others reach down to help him rise. Nights are loud with others sleeping. Between dreams I lie awake listening then fall asleep again into a dream of trees and a face in the trunk of one. I wake with a shock like a fist in my face then remember I've forgotten everything. Pale sunshine through the windows make flickering shadows on the floor, doctors rush past and nurses bring medications.

"Change the channel," the patient with white hair said. "Try another, try something else. Go on, Sapporo. Don't worry about memory. You're a Jap, you don't want to remember. Don't sweat it. That's the main thing." And he laughed and coughed.

I swung my legs clear of the bed and looked out of the window at people entering a glass tower. Between the hospital buildings tall white flowers swayed. I was thin and cool. The flowers were hot.

"Not much to lose, anyway," he said. "I can give you mine in a nutshell." He sat on the bed and bent to scratch his shin. "Hey, you got a nice kid. Hey! Don't listen to the shrink."

As the nurse led me down the corridor I wasn't sure whether what I felt was the contents of my belly or my belly itself or the walls closing in.

The shrink told me the man falling was me, the old couple my parents. "But don't worry. Don't fight it. Tell me how you feel."

"I don't know."

"This is who you are." He showed me a picture. "This is you with your son." Every time we met he showed me the same picture. "Your son is ten. His mother is dead. A foster family is caring for him until you're well." In the picture the boy was smiling. Next to the boy was a man. The shrink told me the names of other things I had forgotten. He showed me a bamboo flute I thought was a stick. He told me over and over I had a son but I didn't know what that meant.

"I have been watching people," I said. "In the garden. They know what to do."

"What might that be?"

"Something private, secret."

"Ah. A mystery."

"Hidden work."

"Yes?"

The boy ran to the entrance of the shelter and back, skipped over my feet, and the green blur of our colliding bags made my vision jump.

"We are early," he said. "The bus isn't here yet."

Shrieking birds landed in the tall tree, in every branch over our heads, and on the wires that ran through the branches. The boy craned his neck and I saw a pulse there, under soft white skin. He was not the embodiment of something I had lost. He was real. We'd been out playing catch. Catch was the past coming out of the sky, hitting my gloved hand.

"Look at the starlings, Dad." We raised our heads and watched the birds unfurl into flight and sweep along the street into the valley between buildings. I felt his small hand in mine.

"I dreamed I found you in a tree," I said.

The boy shielded his eyes with his hands. "When we get home," he said, "it'll be all right. You're stressed. I'll make us some toast. When you remember everything it will be the way it was before."

The starlings were like thoughts I couldn't track; like thoughts they were inventing their world from bits and pieces, each bird carrying part of it; when they converged to use what they'd carried, they vanished in light. Their wings tilted and radiance filled the intersection, tilted again and the day was dark.

"This is our bus," said the boy. He screwed up his eyes. The bus waited, shuddering. "Let's go," he said. "Come on!"

We sat four seats back from the driver. Our jackets were green and we had green bags. In mine were my baseball glove and the ball and my tracksuit. I compared these surroundings to the hospital ward. The sun shone the same but the shadows were bigger. I was attracted to the open mouth of a woman sleeping in the next seat. A voice behind us said, "He's a fucker." Everyone seemed quiet, ready to explode. I wasn't hungry or thirsty, but I needed to piss. A large delicate-leafed tree caught my attention and I kept thinking of it long after the tree had gone. My son gave me a green slip of paper.

"Transfer," he said.

"Transfer," I repeated.

"We can get onto another bus."

"This bus is fine."

He blinked. "This bus will only take us part way."

"I need to piss."

He giggled.

I rubbed the soft green paper in my hand. Like a leaf. I felt heat rising from a dark blue organ in my body. I wanted something. I wanted to be loved. I remembered nothing, nothing earlier than the hospital. My son told me our ancestors were musicians and dancers. He told me I was a musician from Japan. He told me that our ancestors were dancers and that I came here to make money and his mother was dead, my wife, and I was not rich. He told me that when he was small he flew over the Pacific. He told me his mother was an angel who came to him some nights. This was one of many bus rides. Later we brought a bat, but it still wasn't baseball, he said, for baseball you needed a team. We were two animals who were shy of each other. I understood why my wife never appeared to me, even as an angel. It was because I thought and thought about him, only him, trying to learn what was between us. Every day we took the bus to the baseball diamond, past the tree with the delicate leaves. "Mimosa," he said, when I asked what kind.

The branches still fill my mind, the trunk glowing in a river of light, then comes this deep old pain, familiar as breath, from losing the boy. I lose him again every time I think of him, every time I touch the back of my skull to locate the bump, still there. A flicker in my head, the flock's momentum, the birds. A bus with all its windows open and wind rushing through. Pain is the oldest thing about me. I remember clearly how I watched this boy, how I learned that the world, with it's continents and islands and oceans and planets and stars, inexplicably went on, and he and I went on in our own way, just as inexplicably. In those days I had a short soft beard. The black hair on my arm was the colour of my son's hair. We had the same white skin. I believe there must be a reason to forget, just as there must be a reason to keep moving.

In hospital the patient with white hair told me about the sorrow he felt at being alone. He said grief kept him confused. I could see that grief was a metal box in his belly white hot and full of flames. There was a forest around his heart and a dry wind blowing. He showed me a photograph of a goldfish in a glass bowl and as his eyes leaked tears he said life was full of life and that it helped if people got a fish. He said jump in your car and drive to the mall and buy a fish. And he laughed.

In the room I shared with my son the walls were bare. In a drawer were chopsticks, in a cupboard dishes and pots. Others lived in other rooms. Music played loud all day. Broken songs kept me from leaving the room. I don't know why such a simple thing — the sound of a piano — froze me, but I sat in the dark while my son slept and felt every string twang and couldn't move till the music stopped.

One day at the end of summer, after we took the bus to the baseball diamond and he held my hand as we walked beside the chain-link fence to our separate dirt islands, a girl with a camera appeared. When I threw the ball, she aimed her lens and clicked, then opened her eyes wide and scanned, hungry for something else to eat up. We stood in hot sun. I told my son to be still so perhaps she would ignore him. He held the ball to his chest and screamed at her across the field. Her mouth went slack. She looked down at her toe kicking the dust, then smiled up, her eyes the colour of wet earth.

I asked my son if we could buy a fish. We took a bus to a mall and found a pet shop with lizards and spiders and rabbits and kittens and fish and a red female puppy, the last of the litter. "This is what I want," said my son. "This dog." I put both mitts in my bag so he could carry the dog home in his. At the end of the mall was a photography shop where the salesman showed us how to load and work a camera, and on an indoor avenue my son told me to stand next to a tree in a pot. "We can both get in the picture," he said. So I got in the picture with my son, put my hand on his shoulder, and smiled, and looked happy, or so I imagined. When we got on the bus the puppy's head protruded from the opening of the bag and she looked at us, licked our hands. She was skinny. "I think she is beautiful," he said. "She's red like a sunset." He took my thumb and pressed it against the dog's nose. The dog peed in the bag. My son's face was very tender, laughing. I cradled the bag of dog food in my lap. The camera hung round my neck.

"She has big paws. See? That means she'll be a big dog." He tickled her ear. "When I go back to school you must promise never to leave her alone. Promise?"

I couldn't promise anything because I knew so little, but I nodded.

"She can be mine and the camera yours."

On the last warm day at the baseball diamond, the girl with the camera spoke to my son. He showed her our camera. She gave him a picture of me and they both crouched on the brown grass and took shots of the dog.

While my son was at school I wrestled with the dog, listened to the piano playing on the other side of the wall. I heard over the music a man shout, "Go ahead, hate me," and a woman said, "You're so selfish." Music crashed against the wall; a door slammed. The puppy looked at me and I picked her up. Life was fierce. From the window was a view of two steeples, people walking, small as ants. Other lives seemed brutal, yet I was hardly alive, my breathing so faint. I went down the hall and knocked at the door and the music stopped and a young woman answered. She looked at the puppy in my arms. "Yes?" I couldn't speak. I went back to my room and set the puppy down and returned to the window. For five minutes I named all the objects I recognised. I imagined falling again, but falling might break bones, even kill me. Every night I dreamed I knew what I was doing, but when I woke it wasn't true. I wasn't cold at the open window, but I shut it anyway.

My son came home and drank a glass of milk. We sat at the table and made a list of food we would buy. I wanted to say something useful to him.

"What is that song?" I asked.

"Just a song on the piano."

But no. The song was about movement, because stillness was so frightening. I was getting ready, but for what? When the music stopped everything seemed to disappear, everything wanted to vanish, and I wanted to vanish, to throw myself in another hole. I wanted to go back and insert things into my life, but didn't dare stop to do it because the song must keep going or not exist. I could remember no moments between which to insert my things, the things that would make me special and loveable. I wanted to invent things that were in my life before. It was late and I was upset and didn't know what to say and so was silent.

"More milk?"

"No."

We sat at the table and refused to look at each other while it got dark.

When I held my breath I became nothing, the silence still lonely, but as long as I didn't lose myself in thoughts of what preceded the silence and what might come next it filled with the murmur of the night world, the city, a foreign place, which ignored me. My thoughts were getting longer.

On Monday mornings at eleven I met with the therapist to talk about what I was feeling, and how to claim those feelings and recover my past. We sat in silence. He was a nervous man with wild eyebrows and a reassuringly open mouth. He wanted me to say my name. He gave me a pen, asked me to write something, anything, my name. He asked what I wanted to do.

We looked at each other, knees almost touching, and tears streamed down my cheeks. I clutched the pencil and my fingers tingled, my lips were numb.

"Try writing your son's name."

I shook my head.

"What do you feel now? What do you feel?"

A loud crack, as of bone on stone. The leather ball arced high, fell out of a cold blue sky. I was living slow, waiting for a signal. I held the mitt above my head and shut my eyes and cold wind clapped my ears, whistled in the chain-link.

Parabola. Diamond. Ovoid. Field. I was learning words. Traffic hummed and the red dog yelped. Reaching for the ball, I thought of the door of the fridge where my son had stuck photographs of each of us holding the puppy. She was bigger every day. Leaping at the glove, her claw scratched my arm, a long red line, as the ball hit my palm. The sun left the sky and it grew dark and cold. I felt something, a pang. The cloud-moving wind.

At home, after supper, I told my son I was going away. Like a small soldier, trained and full of confidence, his hands at his sides, fingers lightly curled, he stood to attention and looked at me. "You'll have to come back at night," he said.

Neither of us moved.

"You'll have to come back at night," he repeated.

We watched TV. A story about whales and a story about a family. *"I'll never leave you, never ever leave you,"* a person said to another person.

We brushed our teeth, went to bed. I didn't know what to expect, but I woke before morning. There was no moon. Rain gleamed on the road under the streetlights. My son was in a sweat, rolling in his bed, and when I touched him he was not my son but a wild smooth animal in its nest, taut with panic and fight, till he recognised me and settled back to sleep. So I knew what would happen if I went. Part of him would never wake and part of him would never sleep. I was hungry, but didn't know what in the kitchen was edible and what was not; what must be cooked, what could be eaten raw, what combinations went together, what would be satisfying to eat alone. I boiled water, opened a packet.

Very slowly, with each mouthful, daylight entered.

I was born in Sapporo in the islands of Japan and I do not know what that means. Nor do I know whether or not my son grew to resemble me. Sapporo is inland, north facing, on Hokkaido, the northern island. My heart was filled there, ancestor by ancestor.

On TV a man said that the world would end soon. "After the millennium," he said, "wars will escalate, with increasing religious and spiritual motivations. People will run screaming in the streets."

I stood, put my knuckles in my mouth, and looked back and forth from the TV screen to my son's bed. I shut my eyes to his terribly soft skin, and imagined people sleeping, sleeping with their mouths open.

Bright sun in his face, he woke with a sharp cry, one cheek red from the pillow. He said he wanted dark glasses, shades, he said, to keep the sun off his eyes. The sun, he said, hurt his eyes. Also he wanted toys. Today was Saturday and he wanted toys. We went to the mall and bought five squat plastic warriors that he tossed in the cold air, followed with his eyes as they spun, falling, to bounce on the sidewalk. His skin was so fair and pure, his hair so dark. He was hurt, in hiding.

My son arranged a party, food and guests. He said in honour of the red dog and called the photographer from the park and the couple from next door. On the evening I was terrified I was going to leave him, that this was a farewell party. We ate noodles and shrimp and strawberries and pineapple. My son and the dog shared a small bowl. The girl with the camera said she was studying the parks of the city;

she'd finished the pictures, now she was writing stories. "I can't imagine losing my memory," she said. "Every time I develop a print I pretend I've never seen the image before. But the stories are always full of pieces of memory."

"He used to be a musician," said my son.

The pianist looked bitter. "You were lonely. Musicians are always lonely. That's why you lost your memory. That's right, isn't it?"

"She's pissed off," said her husband. "She'll tell you it's my fault. I'm never home. I treat her bad. I only pay the fucking bills. Excuse my French."

"You're both unhappy," said the photographer. "Why d'you stay together?"

"Yeah, well," said the husband.

"When I was a kid," said the photographer, "all I ever did was run away."

"The puppy's not lonely," said my son.

We looked at the dog and at the boy. There was a current between them, a thousand eyes tumbling between him and her.

"Yeah," said the pianist. "She's so cute." She started to hum and tears floated down her cheeks. Her husband stooped and offered the photographer a cigarette. I felt a dance in the room, but didn't know how to start.

A year went by, another summer. Autumn. Winter. When the habit of the land predicts the house beams. When temple bells crack the heart. When the city is a lance and the people blood. When actors do not know what they are doing. When a bend in the road follows the coast and people on the bus lean to the water. When countries are piled like hands one on top of another and a nail is driven through. When, not remembering who you are and waiting for someone with the hope of feeling something grasp you hard, you feel nothing. Then you're going home.

"What's to eat?" the boy said.

"There's a packet, I think."

He boiled water and opened a packet of noodles and we ate. He turned on the TV and I closed the curtains. We watched cartoons, and he fell asleep on the floor. I tried to follow a debate about "The Black Public Spheres in the Era of Bush and Clinton." The commercials made me think of women but I understood nothing. *I'll never leave you, never ever leave you.* I went out into an icy black storm and walked till I was soaked. I sheltered in the doorway of the empty station, watching cars go by streaming with rain while the forest closed in. I listened to the buzz of tires crossing the bridge. The station was like a shrine. How did I know that? A grey animal huddled against a distant wall of Market Square beneath a poster showing the glittering teeth of a young girl's smile. At dawn my sleeping son's forehead was like a moon in the light from the doorway; his mouth was a cave. He'd put himself to bed after giving up waiting for my return. I was drawn to those with open mouths because they seemed unguarded, gentle. I couldn't sleep, though I was certain that if I did I'd dream, and in dreams I'd remember everything. Cooped-up dreams would open my lips to escape.

Monday. Eleven.

"I fell into a hole."

"What's this hole like?"

"Not a cave. An excavation. At the edge the earth was soft and slippery. Inside not so soft. Dark."

"And when you fall? As you're falling?"

"A woman is turning away and a man is turning toward me."

"What happens?"

"I stare into the stars. I'm afraid I'm dying."

"Are you afraid of death?"

"When I touch my son, his skin, it's something I can't understand, so fragile. How will he survive?"

"That is what it is to be a parent. That is a common experience." His eyes narrowed. "Let's talk about death."

"My father had a shovel. His father had a shovel. In the ruins a university was established. There was a symphony orchestra that played western music. My son has read about it. Sapporo was built by Americans on the ruins of the old town."

"You know that Sapporo is where you're from. It's not your name."

"I don't understand the difference."

"Do you remember your wife's funeral?"

"If I remember will I be myself again?"

Trees surrounded the bus, crows in the bare branches, crows screaming. I didn't trust the trees or my son's stories. Inside the bus I was trembling. My parents had finished digging; I was about to begin. I had a past, since the hospital, and another past, and couldn't recognise anything from that other time.

Mimosa. All that I was leapt out with the blood. I wanted to crawl back into my wound. My son was the place my wound had healed. Piano. Dog. Photograph. Words I don't know what to do with.

My son's arms holding the bat got stronger every time we played and he seldom missed the ball. My eyes squinted into the low winter sun. The dog, full grown now, found shelter from the icy wind under a leathery tree in a corner of the field near the bleachers where young people in parkas tried to coax her with orange food. But she was a shy dog. Though she smiled deeply at everyone, mouth wide, breathing quickly, she stayed out of reach. She ran across the field, wind combing her fur, toward the bright yellow coat of the woman behind the chain-link. The woman waved to me so I went to her and we watched my son chasing his dog. Later, in a room behind one of those windows that till then had reflected only sky, I crawled into the spaces she made for me — her soft mouth, cunt. Afterward she talked about dying. I inhaled a feather and sneezed. I curled my toes and tried to bury myself in her arms. The spaces got bigger and made a large empty place where I stretched to catch the ball. The wind sang. The ball spun. I heard my son laugh and saw the stitching around the ball. The flight was joyful, not exactly a bird or the ghost of a bird, something finer, less known.

The woman said she was happy, even when we said goodbye.

My son wore his shades and mittens and followed me slowly while I carried our bags to the bus. We cashed our cheque at the bank, then bought rice and vegetables and more plastic figures. As we walked down the road he tossed them in the air. He made up stories about the new warriors. The way they fell delighted him and he tried to tell me why, some special way of spinning they had. "Who was that?"

"I don't know," I said. "Would you like to meet her?"

He shrugged. "If you hold them like this, and you throw them ... "

I watched what left his hand and fell to the ground, watched him gather them again.

At home, while I put food into cupboards, he sat in the bathtub singing to his soldiers. I could smell the woman on my skin. I'd stretched, covering her, until I felt blood in my ears. My muscles were sore. I stood at the window and heard buses pass with a sigh. Out in the dark couples talked, holding on to one another, marching the street and laughing, blowing smoke from open mouths; a blind man with a dog stood at the curb. I didn't know the song my son was singing. The cold glass on my palms and the light that spilled from the window over the people down in the street were veils my heart swam under. I couldn't believe that the blind man and the dog were still waiting.

Monday. Eleven.

"I wake up crying."

"Ah. Yet you seem happier."

"Perhaps I remember something."

"Tell me about that."

"It's strange and familiar at the same time. It's love, I think. Do I love my son?"

"Do you?"

"If I do it doesn't mean anything because I don't know who we are."

"Who might you be?"

"Nothing. I don't know who we are."

How? Why? The fridge magnets were coloured questions falling into the mouth of the leaping red dog. The dog was the colour of blood and so were her heart and the heart of my son. I was a fraction of all the beating and singing and leaping. I was the next whooshing bus. One breath taken, one released. If I was a puzzle, then what kept me from remembering solved me. A pigeon crooned on the roof. A child's skin was sensitive, food was scarce, and I was afraid of crows. How scared I felt. I couldn't measure the distance between me and my son, couldn't measure the music or the time of day.

He came home from school and was stuttering, upset about something but wouldn't tell me what. He threw his warriors into a corner, marched over to me and started crying. I held him. He said he wanted to watch the World Series video. Late that night I lay with him till he went to sleep. The TV said it would snow. The TV said: You are your own prophet. That's all, folks. My heart floated on a tide as separate from oceans as oceans were from the moon. I watched it rise full like a warrior, like the ball from the bat, the stone from the hole. I knew then that winter would become another summer, that leaves jump out of trees, and home is what we fall asleep into. Just as I was about to dream, the piano music began in the next apartment, and the buses were sheets of light riding the silences of the angry player, the seats occupied by women with open mouths. Dangerous branches already burred with buds tangled the window.

I fucked the woman in the apartment again and felt better. She wanted me behind her. Afterward she made coffee.

"I can't leave the building." She took a picture from a drawer of a bride and groom. "Mom and Dad," she said. "They died a week apart — bless them. Don't they look innocent?" She stood up, held her cup in both hands as she circled the room. "Don't they?"

I went back to my son. The tree the dog sat under had bunches of long needles. My son had gathered these and made a pattern on the dirt path. He and the dog were shaking with cold. We walked home and went to bed. Night passed. I couldn't sleep so I got up and stood naked at the window, my body like a fast river. The first bus of the morning freed the crows to scream on bare trees. Off the coast of the continent a whale surfaced, blowing. My son slept on. Everything seemed fleeting and beautiful. All the pictures slipped from the fridge and landed, with a clatter of magnets, on the kitchen tiles. I opened my mouth to let in the first light.

The welt on my forearm from the red dog's claw had faded to a white line, then vanished. I think of that line. I remember it still. My son snored in the next room. I stuck the pictures to the fridge again. They belonged to his world that, like mine, would end. The dog's tail thumped as I touched the door handle, her eyes pleading.

I walked downstairs and out of the house. The streets were deserted at that hour, before the sun was up. As I passed, I felt seeds struggling, containers of vivid green, in the cracks in cement between buildings. My son would wake to empty rooms and the red dog, warriors on the windowsill, two mitts in green bags.

Days and months are travellers of eternity. So are the years that pass by.

All this was long ago and far away.

I walked through the darkest, coldest day, and boarded a ferry that took me to the mainland where I crept through suburbs, past new tract housing, through villages appended to highways that carried traffic between the coast and the interior, eventually into spring drizzle and farmland where heavy fields shone with rainbows and birds in sunshine sang out. The cars and trucks roared as if to push me back, people yawned and nodded behind their windshields. This is how I left my family; this was the end of my life.

Two

THE DOCTOR WAS TALKING TO HIS father who lay in bed. The boy felt himself pushed forward across the shiny tiles by the nurse's hands on his shoulders. His father wore a bandage on his head and his eyes were empty. The boy doesn't know what to expect because even though his teachers and his new parents and this nurse are nice, they have not told the truth about what happened and can't tell him what will happen next. What he knows is his father has fallen and is sick with amnesia and his best friend Stephen has moved to the Ukraine and he has a new baseball glove and it's okay, probably, maybe, maybe it's going to be okay because his dad looks pretty good, the same as he used to look, almost. The doctor crouched and said, Try the glove. Show him your glove. The boy felt the nurse's hands on his shoulders. He looked at his father, at the doctor crouched by the bed. Afterward, when he was walking away with the social worker, he heard his father say the name of the city where he was born.

"What did he say?" said the doctor.

"Sapporo," the boy whispered.

"Sapporo," said the nurse. "I think he said Sapporo."

A long time later, when the father got out of hospital, the boy met him at the front desk and they walked across the street to the bus stop and went home.

They lived together for over a year. They didn't see many other people, but often took bus rides, to the mall, to the baseball diamond. He is being good, as good as he can, because although it was sometimes fun living in a house with two adults and three other kids, actually he hated it. It wasn't fair. His father, who had lost his memory, never told him anything, had nothing left to tell, and when the boy asked for a story—

"You are something I have lost," said the father. "That's all I know. You have told me that."

"Which do you like best?" he said. "The glove or the bat?"

The boy ran in and out of the bus shelter and starlings shrieked in the trees and he craned his neck to watch them fly over the street. The bus waited. Those birds were fast and his dad looked happy so he shut his eyes and captured this flying and shrieking, his dad smiling, the big purring bus, the driver waving them aboard. He put his hand in his father's hand and screwed his eyes almost shut and went ahead up the step and asked for transfers. So if his father wouldn't tell stories, he would tell them, and this was even better, maybe, maybe, because he was a good, a pretty good storyteller. His mother was an angel who told him stories when he was asleep, like about their ancestors who were dancers, and when he told his dad that turned into a long tale.

His dad asked about a tree and the boy said, "Mimosa." That was a short tale. They rode out to the baseball diamond and he held tight to his father's hand all the way to the pitcher's mound. He let go and stepped back. He ignored the tears gleaming in the man's eyes. It was a hot day and the dirt was dry and yellow and he loved this, all this, most of all this backing away from the mound and his dad who still didn't know how to stand properly. He loved his bat and holding it to his shoulder and facing the pitcher. He gripped the bat till his knuckles were white, and the man stood in the sun and polished the ball on his pants, and when he pitched the boy hit the ball hard, a great hit, and began to run the bases. A woman with a camera took their picture. Father saw her and stopped in the dust and didn't even try to chase the ball, and the boy was really mad so he swooped up the ball and held it to his chest and yelled across the field at the woman.

"We have been playing baseball," Father told the clerk at the camera store in the mall. "We need a camera to take pictures." They went to the pet shop and bought a red puppy. How can this happen! Oh how can this happen? The boy carried the dog in his bag. Her head stuck out of the opening and she licked their hands. She was a cute dog, red like a sunset. Everything is wonderful, even though Stephen is gone and his father sometimes stares at him for hours, and even though he doesn't like to think about the future, even the next day, this moment is perfect. On the bus home he took his father's thumb and pressed it against the dog's nose. The dog peed in the bag. So funny the way people smile when a boy laughs.

"She can be mine and the camera yours," said the boy.

After school the boy and the dog drank a bowl of milk. He was thinking of a story to tell his dad about a boy, a boy in Japan, a story from a library book about a boy lost in the woods who finds an iron book. ... The father sat at the table and wrote lists on a piece of paper. "What is that song?"

"Just a song on the piano."

They put the dog's pictures on the fridge, of each of them holding her, then with the window open and rain coming in, the dog asleep in her box under the table, her claws tapping the kitchen floor, they sat and looked at the pictures. The boy took out his library book and told the story, then told the father about Sapporo and the northern island till it got dark, then they watched TV.

One night that fall the boy arranged a party. It was a party for the red dog. He made invitations out of cut-up milk cartons and delivered them by hand and the people said, Aren't you grown up? And he said, Thank you, can you attend? The girl with the camera came, so did the pianist and her husband from next door. They ate noodles and shrimp and strawberries and pineapple, and the boy wanted to know which they liked best, and the girl with the camera took pictures of everyone. The boy and the dog shared a bowl of beer. He put underwear on his head and danced and couldn't stop hooting until the pianist said, Are you an owl? And then he felt sick and everything went quiet, until the girl with the camera said she was taking pictures of the parks of the city, which made the pianist look sad, which made her husband yell and swear at her. Father said, "I forgot everything." The puppy ran round yipping and yapping, yipping and yapping, and wouldn't let the boy hold her. When the guests got up to leave, she threw up.

In winter it got dark early. The boy made supper. He boiled water and opened a packet of noodles. The father told him he was going away. The boy thought about that. He looked at his father and remembered the hospital, his dad in bed looking at him with dark empty eyes, and remembered that he hadn't thought about Stephen for a long time. He really wanted to know the secret in the iron book; he wanted to run; he wanted to be lost in the forest and find a treasure, a real treasure, not something secret that might lead you into life before you were ready. He turned on the TV and Father closed the curtains. They watched cartoons and, when the noodles were cold, they ate, brushed their teeth, and went to bed.

"You'll have to come back at night," he said when the lights went out.

He was in a sweat, rolling in his bed, and someone was holding him down, trying to get him to tell the secret of the iron book, and he was furious, till he recognised his father's arms and settled back to sleep.

He woke grumpy, one cheek hot from the pillow, one cheek freezing from the open window. The father stood in the doorway and repeated that he was going away. The boy said he wanted dark glasses, shades, he said, to keep the sun off his eyes. And toys, he said. He wanted toys.

"First food?"

"No. Toys."

"You will be late for school."

"It's Saturday."

The father nodded and padded out of the bedroom. The dog followed.

They went to the mall and bought five warriors, and the boy tossed them up, watched them spin and fall. These five will tell him the future — this one that way, that one arms wide, this one apart from the rest, that one bad guy, this one king. He kept an eye on his father and the traffic, but he tracked every shadow on every warrior's face.

All the following summer they went to the ball field and in the evenings watched TV. In September when he went back to school the man didn't buy him any new clothes or give him lunch or money for lunch, and he spent the middle of each day walking around the playground in the golden leaves, the soggy leaves, in his plain dirty white wet sneakers, watching all the kids in the bright lunchroom laughing and being friends. They played catch one last time on a cold sunny day near the end of November. The boy's grip on the bat was strong and he hit every ball high, and the father closed his eyes and held the mitt above his head. The red dog yelped and jumped at the glove. The father smacked the dog and she ran under a tree near the bleachers. The father threw down the glove and crossed the field and went into an apartment block.

The boy waited. School no good. Friends no good. Teachers okay. Stephen no good. Dog good. Dad no good.

The dog joined him and they huddled together. He pitched the ball and the dog retrieved it. The boy said ha. The dog wagged her tail. The boy put on his shades and mittens and told the dog the father was gone forever.

But the father returned and carried both bags while the son held the dog's leash. The father cashed a cheque at the bank, then bought a sack of rice, a case of dog food and a bunch of vegetables, then he bought the son five more warriors from the drug store. As they walked home the boy tossed the warriors way up so they hardly spun. They looked ready for anything as they fell. At home, while the man put food into cupboards, the boy sat in the bathtub singing to his soldiers a slow song, like the one from next door that made his chest hurt, a slow sad song as loud as he could sing, but no one came and the water got cold. That night when a whale surfaced off the coast of the continent, all the pictures slipped from the fridge and landed on the kitchen tiles. The son heard the dog thump her tail and the man whispering, then he fell asleep again. There were nine warriors scattered on the windowsill.

It took the boy and dog a week to finish the vegetables, and after that they ate rice and dog food. When he went back to school he forgot about the dog during the day. He tried talking to the other kids, tried playing with them, but nobody liked him. At home he cleaned up the dog's mess and held her in his arms and they rocked together. They ate and slept and watched TV.

On Saturday, the landlord came round and the boy said his father was back in hospital, and on Monday morning a social services woman came to his classroom and spoke to the teacher, and the teacher called him out and they all went into the principal's office. He said Rose and Webster were looking after him. He said Rose and Web next door were

looking after him and that was good. They said someone
would come to see him; this evening, they said, tonight. The
boy didn't get home till it was almost dark and he and the
dog went out right away and walked for hours. They walked
through the sleet and got home freezing and shivery and
watched infomercials. The boy threw up in the toilet and
the dog tried to eat the stuff.

He didn't go to school. He and the dog stayed in bed all
day, curled up together, and when it got dark they went out
and stayed out as long as they could. Rose was the pianist and
her husband was Webster, and Webster said to call him Web
and to be cool and gave him some cans of food to eat with the
rice. Webster was gone a lot of the time and Rose let the boy
watch her practice, sometimes way after midnight. It was
nearly Christmas, nearly morning. The boy came in and sat
on the floor and Rose played, but after a while she started
crying and her music got mixed up and stuck. The boy asked
where was Web. Rose said he was travelling. The boy said
his father was travelling. She said her father had travelled
too. She went to the fridge and came back with chips and
dip. She said it was almost the end of the century and she
wanted something new to happen. That's why she had her
hair cut short. He said that was cool. She gave him an icy
Coke and the bubbles were almost too much, and he almost
cried, almost. She told him a social worker had been looking
for him, and someone from the school, a young guy with
a frown, some teacher, had come asking questions. When
he didn't answer, she asked him what he liked, what did he
really love? The boy said he was going to change his name
to Star, short for Starling. He said his father wasn't really

travelling but was at a special hospital where people learned how to remember things. Rose said yeah, Web wasn't really travelling either, he was nowhere. Star said it was far away, the hospital. Rose said yeah, she wished she was, far away, wished she was far away, far away.

When Web walked in the door, she looked surprised, then happy, then scared. Web talked about deals and crossing the border and street price. Star watched Web and Rose shoot up, and it was the first time he'd seen such a thing. He thought they were going to forget everything, or get mad at each other, but instead they became nicer and nicer. They sat on the couch and put their arms round each other and told him to go get his dog, he could just this once bring his dog into their apartment and heat up some pizza in the microwave, that would be okay, wouldn't that be fine, fine as fine sugar? So that's what he did. The dog was so excited she messed on the floor, but Rose just lifted her arm slowly and said get a towel from the laundry and mop it up, and Web smiled and said go ahead, boneheads, eat the whole pizza, eat the whole damn thing. Web and Rose lay on the floor and laughed at the boy and dog eating pizza. Then they started to have sex in the bedroom and left the door open so Star could see what happened but nothing much happened. The dog fell asleep with her muzzle in the boy's lap. Web and Rose got very sick, and seemed to be asleep but were dead.

Star closed the bedroom door. He slept through Christmas bells and wind beating on the building, every night sweeping the dog's shit into a corner of the RoseWeb kitchen, every day making a new plan. He watched the trees outside the window and thought about a construction site he used to pass on his walk to school. The workers had stopped building and it was all boarded up, but through the cracks he'd seen a big big hole with a few pools at the bottom and some cement walls people had written on.

He found boards and plastic and fixed up a roof where two of the walls joined, broke into a thrift shop and filled a shopping cart with clothes. It was a clear night and late, yet everyone in the city seemed to be having a time, mostly a good time, though some looked lost like him. It was New Year's Eve, the end of the century, and no one paid him any attention. He filled carts one after another and wheeled them to his new home and piled the clothes high till he had a dry nest for the two of them, for himself and the red dog. They stayed in that place a long while, going out only to hunt food and beg. When the boy got sick the dog hunted alone, sometimes disappearing for the whole night, and Star always hoped she'd bring back a thing he could eat, but she never did. He grew thin. Once she was gone for a couple of days and after that she'd often be gone days at a time. Star was visited by rats and rising water and monsters that gushed blood. Cracks in the cement writhed and hissed. When his fever cooled and he felt okay again, he was as thin as his own bones. He went to find food. He made short trips and shared his food with the dog when he got back. If she wasn't there he saved it for her. He told her they seemed to be going different places and she better take care of herself.

In the warmer days, she stayed with him and had three puppies and one of them died right away. Soon after that she and the two puppies left.

The construction workers returned in the spring and he had to find another place. There was an alley right down town that a breeze ran through all summer and had a wall that heated up in winter. Star lost track of time and used to think he saw the red dog's pups, maybe even the pups of her pups, slipping by in the distance, never close enough to touch. He heard them barking at night. The red dog herself he only saw in dreams, alongside his mother, walking in a park, all lit up.

He found a pink lighter and spent a year burning things. He set fire to garbage and shacks and drunks and cars and offices and money and food and hair and the dead.

The Gorge was a winding river, a valley with paths and chain fences. This was his bathroom and his garden; restaurant alleys were his kitchens, his pharmacies, and adults were his clients and dupes.

He did drugs and sex and stopped talking. He slept through a whole winter and woke up and remembered his father. He started to forget things. He forgot what sex he was, forgot he was a child, forgot his family, forgot he was alive and supposed to die. He remembered his way in the alleys even on the darkest night, even when he was stoned. And who he could trust, who he could rip off, who to fear.

He found other children.

Their closed eyes made night, their sex parts made weather; they showed their bellies to the sun; their legs owned the street. Their names were birds'.

THREE

AN OLD MAN DIGGING A DITCH beside the road called out, "Where you headed?" and when I said I didn't know, he said, "Try the desert. It's along this road. You'll get to it. I tried it once. Didn't do a thing for me, though some people swear by it." The soft sky clamped his shoulders as rain began to fall. The grass in the field was brown, fresh green showing through. A dense wall of trees ahead held radiance, a silver light shining inside the forest. The wet road gave off a warm smell. "Off you go," he said. "Something wrong? Do you need something?"

I tried to concentrate on the nearest huge trunks, the splayed, leafless, leaning branches, edge-lit black. "A place." I tried to imagine who I really was, deep down.

"That so." The old man leaned on the spade. "I was a sapper in the army. That's how I came by the digging. Digging's the only easy thing now." His teeth were flecked with red. Heavy soil clung to his boots and shovel. "This isn't mine." He gestured all round. "I have to acknowledge that. God knows. Maybe you know who it belongs to?"

"I don't think I've been here before," I said.

"My mistake. I see you now." He nodded. "Desert's down along the way you're headed. Unless it's moved. Some say they don't stay put." The man positioned his shovel, then jumped on the shoulders of the blade. Straining back, he levered to the surface a moist clump bristling with worms. He stepped away, grunting and wiping his face. "I can't help noticing you're not taking a whole lot along. That's wise. Me, I had a shitload of stuff. Took me days to put my camp together, with all the crap I lugged around. Had a sweet little home wherever I went but, like I say, the whole desert thing, complete waste of time. Give me a piece of wet dirt, a spade and a drink of water, and I'll show you a happy man."

So I kept going. I didn't look back. I didn't want to hear any more because anyone could tell me what to do. I was young. Although I already knew life was sweet and bitter and had to do with loss, and though some moods I wanted things — birds, trees, ideas — and other moods I didn't, I didn't want to hurt any bird or tree or idea by trying to catch it or dig it out or own it. My father, if I knew him at all, would have been like this farmer, with eyes fastened to the soil, creeping like a turtle.

In the ditches grew yellow flowers out of water thinly flowing. A mass of pink worms lay by the road edge, and over my head, as I entered the forest road, tiny new leaves flared, already green, bright as they'd ever be. I had nowhere to go and had been somewhere I wasn't reluctant or anxious to put behind me, so I walked slowly into the breathing afternoon, and my heart opened the road, and the road opened my heart wider. Two sparrows sang in a bush charred and shiny. It would be even darker where I was going, past an old oak, then another, then a multitude, up a hill to the top, to the horizon, where in a clearing I saw the last of the day's sun beneath a bed of clouds pushing the world's rim. Awake and dreaming of oceans and islands, I was in the region of black ghosts and ditch diggers, and down below a farm piano tinkled but otherwise the country was asleep. Then I heard the bark of a dog and in the distance frogs singing, and headlights swept the silence. The whoosh of a car got me looking at my walking feet, these loveable feet, and I knew I was retreating from life, and was in pain. But as long as I walked, I thought it would be all right, that something would happen, as long as I just kept moving. I slept under a hedge and kept waking up colder and damper till dawn and the screaming of birds.

The roadside coffee stand had wheels but there was no sign of recent tracks amid the rolling waves of brambles. A woman filled my cup. "Clean nails," she said. "You're old for a student. Shoo, I know. You're one of those foreign exchangers, right? Don't look so worried. It's just a question." She was large and black. On the counter were red-tipped yellow flowers in a vase; the same flowers were unfolding among the brambles. "You're a sweet-looking guy," she said. "Tell me something about yourself."

"I have pictures," I said.

"Lay them on me," she said. "You're surely a heartbreaker."

"This is my son," I said.

She held the snapshot to the light. "Hmm."

"This is his dog. This is the baseball field. This is the pianist."

"Yep," she said, "Yep."

"I heard there's a desert up ahead."

"That's true," she said. "Oh, but it's a ways. And you look tired. I have a shack back of here. You're welcome to rest your bones. Business is slow these days."

I felt the pebbles and twigs underfoot: my boot soles were getting thin, and hours later, still in the country of oaks — no leaves yet, no flourish, no display of energy — I still felt her behind me, mile after mile, sticky and plump, this confusing woman behind me, and then I was in a trough, the road passing between smooth rock faces, the air still, and the woman was gone. I wasn't sure whether I was going under or the cliffs were rising or night was already thick, but all of it was welcome. Then I heard the clatter of hooves at a gallop, then silence, and I raised my eyes to the band of sky to see a shape fly cliff to cliff above my head, a black amazing shape, neither earthbound nor celestial, but huge and suddenly gone. Pebbles clattered on the path. The hooves resumed and quickly faded. I lay down on a bed of moss under a black outcrop and went to sleep. Woke briefly to the scream of a cat. Slept again and woke at daybreak from a dream of a woman bending over me with love in her eyes and felt the loneliness of a place where no one lived.

So I walked out into sunshine and shadows, every day the emptiness the same, every sleep different yet the same, every dream different yet the same. A flap of wings. A woman touching my face. My son with a lick of hair stuck to his temple and his eyes shut. At dawn there was no colour, at sunset only colour. But I did not stop and did not die.

"Hey you! Hey! You're going the same way as me. I've been on this old road lots of times, never seen you before. Are you sick?"

"Me?"

"Yeah."

"I'm fine."

"This path used to be a logging road. I know all the trails. I'm glad it's spring. Look, that's teasel. That's a dead teasel, tall as me. Last summer it was alive. Hey, you seen my horse?" This child throwing out words like crumbs, skipping at my side. Everything about her was fast. "Charlie, that's his name. That's my horse." I'd been walking along with my chin on my chest, watching for fallen branches, loose stones, roots, shoving through undergrowth, leaping streams. Now we were rushing along the track. "My name's Molly," she said. "There's a clearing coming up. I got these big rocks." She held up the bottom of her sweater. Inside, a collection of stones hung down around her knees. "Soon I'll have to slow up. Charlie got out of his paddock more than a week ago. He's never gone away from me this far."

"I saw a horse."

"A big black horse?"

"Maybe. He was jumping."

"He likes to jump. First time I said hello he jumped a hedge. Jumping is his first nature. Where did you see him?"

"Back there. Where the cliffs almost meet over the road."

"When?"

"A few days ago, maybe. I'm not sure."

She nodded and the stones in her sweater rattled. "I got his scent. We'll catch him up. He loves to run away and for me to follow him and head him home. I guess we should make camp."

We rested on a patch of thin grass by the path. The sun shone for a few last minutes. She was a young wild girl away from her family. She told me her father was a farmer like all the people in the area. She had two sisters and a pig, three dogs, a million cats, a hundred cows and six horses and hers was the seventh and he was always getting loose. Her brown hair was tangled with bits of leaf and straw and she wore dirty overalls and a big sweater the colour of mushrooms.

"My thumb hurts. It's swollen. See? The hardest thing is being tired. Night's scary. But toughest is the cold and when you get wet and when you're hungry too. You feel hungry?"

I shook my head. "Do you know the desert?"

"Sure. There's little flowers, blue and pink, masses of them. They only last a few weeks. I'd never go there, no sir. Stay there is what I mean."

"Do people stay there?"

"No way." She was holding her thumb up to my face. "I hurt it getting over a fence. Then I trapped it with these rocks. Did you ever run away from home?"

"Maybe."

"It's all right. I can keep a secret. My daddy's mean and my mom's depressed, but that's not why Charlie ran away this time. You know something? Most people tell me to shut my mouth. You know something else? I'm pretty hungry. Isn't the air nice on your skin? Nice and cool. I love how it feels on my legs at the end of the day. I swear my belly button's stuck to my spine, I'm that famished. So you got anything?" The girl leaned toward me. "You're weird. You listen. You don't talk, you listen. You listen. You got kids?"

"A boy."

"What's his name?"

"It's getting dark."

"You could tell me his name."

I showed her the picture.

"He's a pretty boy," she said. "Tell me your name then."

"Sapporo."

"Sapporo," she said. "Okay, here's something. When I was a baby I knew the names of the animals and plants. I knew the names of the dead people, the children and the old people, all the grass and rocks, the different kinds of fire. When I was real young I knew the name of everybody. What d'you think of that?"

"How did you know?"

"I just knew them by heart. I guess I figured them out myself."

"Did you forget the names?" I said.

"I forget," she said. "I forget if I forgot. Bet you want to know why I am carrying these rocks. To make a ring for a fire. After the crows go roost and the cows lie down, pretty soon now, it'll get cold. I'm smart as a button, you know. I've got matches. There's a bug." She bent down and put her finger over an ant. "I wonder what it feels like to get crushed, your bones squeezed, everything hurting and you can't breathe and no doctor, no hospital could ever fix you. You hear me, little ant?"

Molly made her circle of rocks while I collected wood. We built a fire and sat warming our hands and the stars came out.

"Here." She pulled a ribbon out of her pocket. "Tie your hair back. I can't see your face. Let's tell stories. First me. I saw a sheep fall off a cliff once. It fell and fell, hit the slope and kept rolling over and over. When it stopped rolling it jumped up and walked away. But it fell out of our land and we never saw that sheep again. What d'you think of that?"

Side by side we dozed through the night and in the morning woke curled up together beside the ring of cold stones. It was grey, with a sky of low-flying clouds, the promise of wind and rain. We set out, but soon the girl said she'd lost Charlie's track, and then we smelled sweet meat cooking. Below, through the trees, we saw flashes of yellow and red and heard voices. The girl ran down a soft slope of pine needles into a clearing enclosed by a derelict fence topped by rusted barbed wire. Piles of fresh-split fir. I didn't want to follow, but I went after her anyway. At the far side of the clearing sat a family under a tarp. "Hi there, Molly," said the woman. "Come have a bite with us. You run away again?" The others laughed. "Come in out of the weather. It's going to pour. Who's your friend?"

The table was old fence boards on stumps. They were eating meat from a camp stove the man tended, adjusting dials and prodding at the charred bits remaining, and smoke rose and billowed under the heavy brown canvas strung between two fir trees.

"Don't be shy," said the man. "We're glad to share what we have. Who's your friend, Molly?"

"He's going to the desert."

"That a fact."

"He's all right," said Molly. "He is quiet."

"You'll get wet out there," said the woman. "Come in and have some meat."

"Deer meat," said the man. "Cougar did the work. We just got lucky."

I squatted inside the tarp and took the plate the woman offered, and we ate together as rain rattled the canvas.

"Where'd you meet this girl, Mister?" the woman said. "I won't ask her because she's not got a clear way of speaking. Her dad and mommy kind of let her wander."

"Spends more time out here in the woods than back home," said the man. "Right, Molly?"

"Thank you for the meal," said Molly. She ran up the scree to the road and gathered flakes of shale and ran back and made a square near my feet. "This is for you," she said. "It means a favourite place, a secret place, hard to get to. You have to climb high and go through snow but it's worth it. It's beautiful. I'll go home with these folks," she said. "Charlie's probably made his way back and is waiting for me. You go through the rocky place, then you get to mountains, okay?"

The other children suddenly quit the table and spun screaming across the clearing. Molly hesitated a second, then she waved to me and raced after them.

"You be back before dark!" called the woman.

"She don't make a heap of sense," said the man. "That's all right. You a father?"

"They've all got something on their minds," said the woman. "Always something they've got to do."

The man got to his feet and stretched. "They don't need us, except for a bit of food and shelter."

"They're not afraid," said the mother. "It's like they know something and are keeping it from us — for our own good. Like they're protecting us."

"That's foolish," said the man.

Next day the forest stopped and the ground ahead was scattered with rocks large and small around narrow fissures. My path led through the broken land. A dead bird with flat feathers marked the entrance to this place. Another bird lay headless in stained dust a short way in. The feathers of the first moist, of the second dry. Perhaps the same bird repeated. Perhaps the bird was both hunter and hunted. Anyway, the idea of parents and their children was with me now and I couldn't breathe properly and my shoulders were stiff. It took days to weave in and out and over the rockslide. Then one morning I heard a tiny uproar, branches rubbing, birds ticking, and stopped in front of a black wall of trees, another forest, but nothing like the last one. I was still without my son, but the road ahead wasn't built yet. As soon as I set foot between the first huge trunks, I was in twilight. A tree had a long gash in the bark from which sap had flowed and hardened, a temple door, and my son's face, or my own face my son's age, was inside the amber.

I thought about windows and trapped birds who died trying to fly out. My feet on the ground were streaming with light, electricity sticking them to the path. I thought about others who had passed along this route. I remembered that the dead live in the living. Only the dead knew I was there with my loveable feet shining in the dark. The forest's texture was my own; both of us were green and spiny, soft brown. My body blended into the quiet light; I was becoming a smooth place in the trees. I'd wait in front of the temple door for all that was needed. With my fingers I traced the edges, the translucent beads, the powdery bark. The beads, sticky beneath the glossy surface, tasted bitter. Wind stirred the fur on my arm and light climbed up past the gate of knees to flood my thighs.

I got down on the ground to arrange the photographs around the base of the tree, and it was as though my life had been spent on all fours: standing was a useless miracle. My belly hung, empty. On all fours, I remembered that the living also live in the dead. Birds and dust were the same. Somewhere in these woods, lost a long time, was an ancient home and an ancient family. My paws, front to back, made two parallel lines. Beneath me was a buried lake and when I stood blue steam rose through my feet, climbed my spine, and when it reached my head it flowed on out the forest canopy and love hung by a thread. Shadows moved. A breeze ruffled the treetops. Inside the gummed-shut door there was no room for anything because everything was ready. No more memories. I was at the bottom and must climb. Whoever I was had chosen one mystery, but the dead and the lost had named me another.

I heard footfalls in the bush beside the path, and then was running the forest's rising floor, lashed by wind and exploding leaves, hair whipping like feathers in my eyes. Every furred and fanged thing raged at the edge of my vision. Roots broke the earth to zigzag like sparked fuses under my leaping feet, while bushes thrust flowers, berries, thorns at my skin. In the centre of this fury, while my fists clutched and snapped branches, I had a quiet ear cocked to the rustle of anger so old and dry it knew nothing of itself. Anger intolerant of held breath, of the blood that fuelled the breath. I caught the whisper and heard it wanted to engulf the world. Bark skinned from wet sinews clung to my palms. The tips of dead trees twanged above the forest. No one would survive. We are born, and live, with an arid song haunting our green ears. As young animals, we expect teeth in our throats every moment and we shove our heads against one another. Later, our hips pump blue light, the bluest light, and we stop time. I felt all the trees line up and my heart led my body, almost a tree itself, out of the woods.

I came to a meadow high above the tree line, and walked through islands of red and pink and yellow and blue flowers. The islands were set in a sea of thick green grass beneath a blue sky. I left a trail of bent grass to the far edge of the meadow where, clinging to the last soil, grew tiny alpine plants: turquoise, ruby, cobalt, sapphire. Lying in the grass, head against a rock, lungs trembling in the sweet thin air, I slept. Night was cold and mist rose from the ground. The light from hazy, millennia-long needles, converged, and I dreamed I was flying in the company of friends.

In the morning I ate shoots of the young grass and studied the largest mountain and began to climb. Snow shone in holes in the early slopes and the going was easy. Hawks flew circles overhead. The peaks soared pure white. As I climbed, the forests disappeared in dense cloud and I entered a frozen storm where the nothing of earth lay against the nothing of sky. Days started thoughts and night stopped them, then dreams visited. The child Molly in a cage, the black woman singing, and the farmer's dance that doesn't fit the song. The moon crossed the sky in hours, then minutes, then in a second, fuller and fuller, the stars pale and the snow blue. I scooped and ate snow. On the dawn of the day I made the summit, I found two green eggs in a crevice and sucked them dry. The wind was freezing. A black lake gleamed in a barren valley on the other side. I farted and laughed, the clouds evaporated, and the world's curve was snagged with icy nipples. I squatted in the lee of a boulder as the sun hauled up the sky, and my bowels moved. A thin moist stool steamed, looped on the scree.

By the shore of the black lake was a long beach of round stones, blue, white, blue and white, brown, brown and white, each with a skein of red veins. The water never stirred. The stones slithered and clattered underfoot. I saw in my reflection in the lake the face of a man far from home, and took off my clothes and swam. I have never been so cold. A large bird flew over, dropping from its beak a round object that splashed and sank. I lay on my back in the lake, rolled over, let out all my breath and also sank, my body crushed by the cold, the surface shining above. When I crawled ashore and collapsed beside my pile of clothes, all was still. The stones drank the lake from my skin. I lay on the beach under a faint sun, my hands turning over pebbles, and watched thoughts rise — warrior, hunter, father. Whatever spun, whatever was spinning, the spin seemed right.

A stream flowed from the lake and I followed it through flat boulders to a narrow channel worn smooth. The water seemed motionless in the trough, a clear window, and it fell — unruffled and glistening in last light, a gelid pillar — over the edge into an abyss, where it vanished in darkness.

I got used to nights in snow caves. Every lake seemed the same as the first, still as oil, every peak was troubled by the same nervous wind. One egg was the same as every egg; I was astonished by the powdery shells unbroken by the sharp rocks that cradled them. Thick mucous with a sweet yolk. The trick was to puncture the yolk for the taste before the jelly slid down the throat.

There were no trees in the region, yet on one lake a tree floated upright, its top branches overhanging the water. When I dipped my fingers, the water tasted of soil. This water was too buoyant for me to swim beneath the surface: it made a perfect ice-mold for the human form. With my face in the water I could see the roots in the blue-green walls of the lake. I remember my eyes were open wide, my limbs were white, and the roots rippled as though alive.

~

I woke in a panic, unable to breathe, everything beyond the shallow cave blazing, thunder hammering the rocks below, lightning stitching the horizon. The storm lasted all day and toward evening I was visited by a bird who darted in to shelter in the warmth between my arm and my side. "What are you doing here?" The bird fluffed its feathers. It's head fell forward, beak open, panting, black eyes watching. Then it hopped into my hand and pecked at a freckle. I can see it now, a green and speckled thing. I can still feel it thrumming.

When morning came, the bird was gone. The clouds dissolved and sunshine glittered off the snow. That night, when I saw in the sky the same pattern of stars as in the bird's plumage, I knew it was time to climb down from the mountains. I had remembered forgetting, but not what was forgotten. Descending was dreadful. What had taken place would never happen again. For instance: the meadow when I reached it was dead. What had taken place had never happened before. My eyes hurt. I was disappointed. Without stopping I plunged down through the wilderness, my mind raw, and every bone with its own pain.

I came to a chasm under a cloud, too far to jump to the opposite edge. There was no way to lose, I'd lost it already. There was no way to lose what I was afraid of. I was afraid of everything, and everything was wrong. I went back to the meadow where the stream had run dry and nothing stirred the dust of leaves and a mountain shade fell on my face. I'd come this far and could go no farther. I kneeled in pine needles and tasted grass and dirt and watched ants, a spider, seven sow bugs in a range of worm casts.

That night I started shaking and couldn't stop. I vomited and shit at the same time. My bowels turned inside out. There was an avalanche and I was near the bottom, and everything I'd been was near the top, and all was in motion. If I let go the world would end. No one would survive. If I gave what I wanted shape, gave myself what I wanted, I would die. I was terrified during the night. The noise of slides kept me awake. It was horrible to wake alone, not knowing what I'd lost, and yet horror was a relief: the earth slowly heating up in the sun's rays and the distance between sun and earth insignificant. I was bright with anguish over the loss of a boy I'd loved more than my own life, a boy I'd never meet again. I will never see my wife again. I can't even remember when we were together and in love. Now this salt, salt in the mouth, this falling off the map. So, what did it matter that I couldn't remember? A lizard watched me and I called, "Silverhide, a hand in the egg fetched you out, didn't it, even though you screwed each toe into the corners of your little room?" I went back to the hospital, the bus, the city. I wove together iridescent feathers, made a veil out of lichen, and danced out of my bones. *He was terrified during the night. The noise of slides kept him awake.* Life meant agony, nothing but. This dancing body at the foot of the mountains was going to die with a star map in its pocket, without hitting the bottom, without going back.

I didn't want to try to jump the gulf, didn't want to let go of everything yet, but I went back to the crevasse and stood at the edge. I'd wait till I knew. Wait till I was strong enough. My feet burned. The idea of leaping burned. I sat down and put my head between my legs and breathed. I didn't want to fail. I stood and turned and took seven strides away from the edge. In the valley of my father's house was a deep well. Behind the east door of the house was a barrel with a clay cup on the lid, sour dregs of whisky in the cup, droplets clinging to the red rim, and under the lid cool water from the well. My whole body was on fire as I ran forward, leaping in an arc. On the desk in Father's room was a flute with mist on the bone mouthpiece.

I was into sky so large and blue above grassland so bald they must have been intimately connected, on a straight prairie road, the mountains behind me, my left foot bloated and full of pain. A town appeared on the horizon, visible only at night, and low cars sped past. I slept in the dry ditches by the highway, wind whining over stubble fields, rattling Styrofoam plates and cups against the leaning fences. As I limped past, cattle on either side struggled to their feet. A truck caromed through dust on a side road and stopped. A hatted figure slouched across and held out a hand. Birds began to sing. I liked the man's boots. It was late in the day and sun shone through the fence and made shadows on the road and the cows gathered at the fence, their faces raised.

"Howdy," said the man. "Reckon you've come a fair distance." He looked around. "Yeah," he said. "Lots of critters about. Where you headed?"

"The desert."

"Hang around a couple of years." He gave a short laugh, then sat on his heels and picked up a fistful of dirt. "Didn't catch where you're from." He sniffed the dust, let the wind carry it away.

"I have lost my family."

The man looked up, then sighed. "You want a drink?" He stood and reached into his back pocket, held out a flask. I tilted the whisky to my lips. The cows' shadows crossed the road, their legs stilts, and we stood on these red, shifting lines. "Small hands," he said. "You have small hands. That ribbon you wear, where'd you get that?"

"A child gave it me."

"Had a girl once wore a ribbon that shade."

"She said she couldn't see my face."

"These are mine." The man pointed the flask. The cows moaned, tails lashing. "You're welcome to cross my land."

"Thank you," I said.

"You bet." The man looked at his hands, shrugged. He walked back to his truck and drove away. Sun struck the wall of a barn. Steam lifted from the pile of shit one of the cows had left behind.

Before night, in a curve of the river, a cougar stepped from soft sand into the fast water. She raised a thick tawny head, feathery ears tipped high, and listened. Her mouth fur glistened with droplets. I imagined the two of us in the black river, swept downstream, clasped in each other's arms. But the cat was all alone and wasn't to be owned, not even in a dream.

After the cougar had finished drinking and gone away the sun vanished, a rooster called, another answered. The highway that evening felt good. In the city I'd find a room and work at some small job. A bus swept by and wobbled ahead along the road. I sniffed at the exhaust fumes, felt a pain in my chest, and imagined lifting my son from his bed. The river curved away. I belched whisky and heard a long flute note. My belly cramped. Irrigation hoses exploded. Wild roses grew near the ditch, and I ate a few. The dirt smelled like rain. I found honeysuckle and ate that. As long as I kept going forward I wouldn't lose my balance.

I'd fallen into a hole my father had dug and hit my head on a rock. In the hospital garden a tree waited for a cavity in the earth. I'd flown across a gulf and injured my foot and started along this road. Wind whipped dust from the barren fields. My nose was dry as a cave. I hobbled down to the river to drink. That night I could smell the city and heard it roar as I lay down to sleep. Its lights no longer twinkled but burned steadily. I thought of my son: that small stranger's lean legs, slender bare arms. I didn't know my own son. Nothing would hold him close and carry him to safety now. I held up my hands. They too were once a child's. I dreamed people were gathering to forgive me, to welcome me back, and woke to a moon and the sound of coyotes yipping. I got up and going, feet on blacktop, arms wide for balance. None of this was to be owned, none of it.

By noon everything looked slick and strange. By late afternoon I felt dizzy and my heart beat violently. I fell down and my son helped me up. We began to run. We were mocked by barking dogs and the spotless sky. Keep that door clotted. We ran, my foot screaming. On one side of the road were trees with spaces in the branches through which wires passed. Then my son was gone and I was no longer running, no longer on the highway, but on an avenue, in a green tunnel between rows of huge trees. The light was thin and remote. Ditches were littered with books and the wind, stronger and stronger, riffled the pages like whispering leaves, and I followed the wires toward the middle of the city where loud music came from open basement windows.

FOUR

STAR SPENT TIME. HE SPENT TIME. Spent time remembering his father, time making money in the park, letting old men play with him while trees swayed in the light. He had his back to the wall and could hear feet running on the other side. He hung with those kids, shooting up. They were shooting up back there. He got them knives, guns. Every night he'd cross the bridge, deal in the city, sleep a while, come back in the morning. He sold them dope, what they needed, till the cops got wind and he had to chill. From this place, his back to the wall and his front to an old guy on his knees, he could see the guy's white hair, thin on top, and his pink scalp. He could see the branch shadows going nuts on the ground and smell new grass from the mowing and piss from the toilet stalls behind the basketball court. Star knocked down the hands pawing at his hips, then came. He had nothing left to say or feel so he pushed the guy over. He could smell rain on the blacktop. The guy spat and crawled into the bushes.

These days his people, even his street buddies, wouldn't trust him. He'd gone too crazy. He flapped and hopped under the tall shiny buildings. Walked up to citizens and started rapping about his dad was a blade, thin and strong, already free, and now what seemed far from him was most his own. He was a blade. He could open up the world, top to bottom, one slash. He was the blade. He could walk into the wound and seal the flesh round him, but they paid no mind, the citizens, or flipped him a coin.

He zipped up and quit the park to see who was visible. He'd been busy studying the warlords. One called Dit had a black Cadillac, and she was cool and the car was cool, and today he was lucky enough to catch her between deals.

"What d'you want to do with me?" he asked her.

"You got nothing makes me want you for nothing," Dit said.

"I got a name."

"You got a sweet little prong and a sad look and you're trouble on the street."

"I can deal," he said.

"Hey hey."

"I can suck. I can run."

"You got ears?"

"What d'you want me to do?"

"Stay out of my way."

"Anything, Dit, anything you say."

"Baby, I don't even want to know your name."

"Give me a job. Tell it to me."

"You want to turn a trick, turn a trick. You want to steal a car, steal a car. I got things to do."

"Come on. People know you."

"Shit, boy. You say you can run?"

"I'm gonna get connected. I'm giving you this one chance, Dit."

"I think you're gonna die, baby, that's what I think," said Dit. "You can't do me nothing. You're gonna die before you've had two thoughts."

That night, Star lay in his alley and looked up at the coloured smoke, the air so hot. The traffic sounded echoey with the heat and the dusk sparkled. He told himself what he knew was a lie. He said to himself that he was a warrior, a wave man with no boss, no family, no fear. He watched people at the end of the alley passing a bottle. They were old and shaky and shouted at one another, then laughed and laughed. Sometimes, he thought, you get tough. Sometimes, Star thought, you get crazy and feel like a steel spike. The sky was jujubes, all that neon, and he felt like grabbing a handful and waking them up, all different colours flying, and hitting, smashing, till he wouldn't see a thing, no more jujubes. Maybe Dit would answer a question or two, if he could figure a question.

Next day, Star met a girl called Robin and got her hooked up. When they learned each other's names they squawked and fluttered. They found a crate of coloured Christmas balls and pitched them against office towers and watched a person walk out of each shower of glass.

"Another one!" yelled Star.

"How do we do that?"

"We're fucking birds!"

"We're making people!"

"Fucking geniuses!" said Star.

They laughed.

"See them?" said Robin. "I mean how they move? That's dope."

"Yeah," said Star.

"Bot people," said Robin. "What things." She threw the last yellow ball; it exploded; nobody came. "I'm hot."

"Me too."

"My cock's askew," said Robin.

"What?"

"My thing's in a knot," said Robin. "I hate the city, and you know what? My hate is true. You ever been in the country? It's cool. Totally."

"Let's go to the Gorge."

"That's not country. The Gorge stinks."

"We can swim. I know a place."

"That's shit. This is all shit. We need to make money. Yow! I need sex, man."

"It's early," said Star. "Let's go swimming."

Star was afraid of one danger, the secret loving and praising of his father. Even in the heat there was a cold place inside. Sleep after sleep he dreamed of his father's return, woke to fresh loss. In dreams he walked through the mall and his dad spoke a strange language and his fingers had turned into claws.

At the Gorge Robin and Starling hung with a young guy who was trying to catch fish with shoelaces strung together and a bent nail. They called him a crazy crazy fuckhead fishboy, and he pretended they didn't exist, but he threw the hook short and his line snagged and they called him Goose, and together they decided to be a gang of birds. They swam in the brown junky water and splashed and screeched, held their breath and went under, went down where they found old boots in the silt. Shivering wet and grinning, they built a pile of soggy leather on the grey beach and Star said that what he loved most was old shoes, and Robin said what she dug most was small eyes, and Goose said he liked nothing better than laces, and Star said they needed more birds. Robin said she had a bird she didn't need, and Goose said what? and Star said Robin was a she with a cock. Robin said yeah and Goose said what? Star said he needed his bird to love everything in the world to be loved. Robin shook her head and said there was too much garbage and too many citizens. Goose said garbage stank. Star said shoes, man, shoes, shoes had everything. Said give me a shoe with a good sole, good tread. Give me tongue, said Goose. Right on, said Robin. The three of them went uptown and Dit said they looked fresh as baby rats looking for a bite. Robin said they were hungry for sure. Star said they needed nobody. "We are birds."

"We are free as music," said Robin.

"We are spicy," Goose said.

And they were magic. They were buddies. They had names.

Dit smiled.

"Man, did you see her," said Robin.

"We hooked her," said Star.

"Who is she anyway," said Goose.

"Yeah, who is she anyway?" said Star.

"So what are we gonna do?" said Robin.

They got wrecked together, hours of freebasing junk chased with coke, and decided to build paradise. This was paradise. The alley, the city. They were birds, a tribe of birds, this was paradise.

"Mercy, mercy," said Goose.

"Let's split," said Star. "Let's split. Farewell my wife and children!"

"Farewell, brothers," said Robin.

"We split," said Goose, "we split, we split."

FIVE

ON THE FIRST DAY I STOOD on the street in a crowd of shining faces gathered to watch the moonrise, and we stared as the pale disk surged out beyond the city lights. Satellites crossed overhead, trains rumbled under the streets, crews lay cables beneath the oceans. These people were reining in chaos. Laying ghosts, getting comfy. There was no sign of recognition in the eyes of those I met.

I worked nights at a battery, grading eggs. When the hens jumped about in little cages, their red combs flopping, I saw something dark, an intimation of death, and when they scratched at the floor, scratched and scratched, walking in circles, the scales on their yellow legs made me dizzy, and the pattern looked like life itself.

At dawn as I walked home I caught glimpses between buildings of patches of forest in the wide moonlit plain. In my room I undressed, lay down to sleep, and once again was in the mountains, swimming the lakes. Places were easier than people. When I couldn't sleep I ran into morning rushhour, spent the whole day cruising streets. People wore

scarves. Shop windows displayed bright things. I loved a
stainless steel pot. I bought a scarf, the pot, Christmas
ornaments.

I spent shifts in a trance, staring at the chickens, finding
my image in the hub of those black shiny eyes as I collected
their warm smooth eggs. I learned to cluck softly. I wanted
to let the birds loose in parks, where they'd scratch holes
to lie in during the day and roost at night in low branches
of the trees. I boiled stolen eggs in the pot and ate them on
buses, on sidewalks, in movie houses at matinees. I watched
the film once through, and for the second show sat back and
studied the audience to find out how to organise my face. At
home I arranged my overalls on the bed, my ornaments on
the floor and table, hung scarves on wall hooks or over the
backs of chairs. I wanted to be involved in a small mystery,
an unexpected thing. Start some new pattern perhaps: my
room was subtly changing, but no one could see what I was
up to.

I watched movies and decorated my room and stood on a
busy street jostled by children and parents, young and old
couples. Like the chickens, I seldom slept and was always
alone, often in bright light, and clumsy. In the depths of
winter I was caught in the chest by the tine of a forklift
shifting crates of eggs. In the depths of winter I travelled
on crowded buses and sometimes got a seat beside a tired
commuter, and sometimes she'd fall asleep, rest her head
on my shoulder, open her mouth so I could feel her breath
coming and going as we careened through the dark and
ice. In the depths of winter I plunged through rush-hour
crowds with new ornaments in my pockets, a silk scarf

unfurling from my neck, and was doubled up by the pain in my side: the cracked rib. When the pain eased I looked around. Surely this rushing and collecting wasn't the point of life? No one noticed my distress. I went up to a big car with smoked glass and slipped my fingers under the handle. I needed to explain to someone how I felt, that my loneliness was a wide-awake thing, that I needed to sleep, needed to be touched. The driver yelled and drove away.

Perhaps I was biding my time, waiting, maybe, to remember it all completely.

The population of the city was growing. Inhabitants built their houses out into the plain, all the way to the foothills, where the forests were dwindling. During the summer I slept less and less, a few hours around dawn, then wandered the new streets, sniffing at earth smells, clay and sawdust. On the edge of these developments, I watched yellow excavator arms claw holes in the ground. On the hottest days, when fumes wavered in the air, I hoped construction workers would faint into my arms so I could break their fall and they'd wake up full of gratitude.

Asleep in my room I dreamed about going back, but woke and realised it was too late. I'd left my son the way you leave a chair. The journey had been years ago and the boy would be grown and full of blame. The apartment overlooked a carpet of roofs. It was midsummer, toward evening. Direct sun struck the window. I sat on the edge of the bed. Sweat pricked my skin. I leaned over and picked up a clump of dust from the floor, walked to the open window and let it float away. Doves or pigeons, points of white light, wheeled around a distant glittering tower. Sun poured in. My chest hurt with a pain deeper than that from moving crates. What would my boy be like? There were years of dust in the brilliant room. I picked up my broom and began to sweep. Yesterday I'd watched kids in the park and something had yawned as big as the city. All the beaks of all the caps turned toward me because I'd picked up the ball. I'd kept my life simple. I'd kept moving. They were waiting, these boys and girls. But always, just like that, the world would turn away, the game resume without me; my hands would be empty.

One day I felt the shadow of someone caress my back and turned to see a man stepping quickly out of sight. Over the course of the next few days I caught the same man right behind me or following at a distance. Discovered, the man would hide or stand still. The city had been indifferent to me. I'd felt unobserved, safe, my life a seamless round in which no fragment could find a lodging point. Now all was transformed. Dry wind blew from the mountains and sucked moisture from every lawn, grey soil drifted over the toes of my shoes. I stumbled in a daze from work to home and nothing was familiar. The journey between sleep and waking seemed fraught with peril. Now there were tears on my cheeks. As the days went by, I made a habit of spinning to catch the stranger. I was in a panic of anticipation. No one had ever (had they?) considered me this closely, this long. The first time I met the man's eyes — he was wearing a red turban and a blue shirt, leaning against a yellow car — the background blurred, green trees waving against a white sky, and the street rocked like a liner on a rolling ocean. The entire city pulsed under a dome of cloud. The man's face grew indistinct, his mouth opened, and he seemed to crouch against the car, as if needing support, his right hand cradling his ear. His eyes were brown, dreamy, and he seemed enthralled by me. Although I could barely focus, I sensed a flaw in the man's back, a hump or crook, and when this amazing creature broke and ran, I knew I had lost something vital. After that, life was a series of stops and starts, every moment a transition, nothing in itself. I was followed and nauseous and ecstatic, or else alone and feeling abandoned. Day, night, changes of weather, season, all of it threatened to obliterate this relationship, which was premised on something hidden, and which promised a reality beyond any I'd dreamed. Whatever it all meant, I could not speak to this man, couldn't bridge the gap between us by any act of will.

Then one day I saw the man's hand, beautiful, dark and fleshy, on the back of my bus seat. "I can give you everything in the world," the voice whispered. "See out there? What would you like?" I stared at the passing streets and felt nothing, only the gaze of those brown eyes. "Didn't I promise always to look after you?" He whooped and cackled. The other passengers turned in their seats.

Animals looked out of people's faces. Animals and children looked out of faces of the old. I stared at the hungry eyes of kids looking out of animal faces, and at animals looking through children's eyes. Children and animals and the old saw ways to be in the body of the world. The child in the tree was beyond the generations. In the library people moved among the stacks, their faces soft. A hand stirred at a table by a window. I wanted to think, wanted to put this right, put it all right.

The man killed a boy on the edge of a field mined for development. The man killed a boy and made sure I saw him: on the edge of the field, out of the city — fresh tarmac crescents, half-built houses — between an abandoned car and an old rotting wood cart. The quick killing: a scream, flurry of violence. I turned in time to see the fatal blow, and I felt sick. The man was a blur of motion, somehow twisted, somehow deformed, but human as he emptied the dead boy's pockets, put everything into his own pocket. And afterward between us came the same dreaminess we'd shared before. We were reluctant to leave the field. We shuffled about between the cart and the car. I wondered if this was a creature, not a person. "What is your name?"

The grunt was a kind of answer.

"Where do you know me from?" I needed both of us to be human; I wanted nothing to abstract this monstrous shared privacy.

"See what I got? It's not much." He showed me a knife, lighter, coins, some shells. We gazed down at the dead boy. "A happy child. Mother's boy. Genius maybe?" The words in his throat as rich and dark as soil.

And just like that the tide turned and I began to dog the murderer; I would not see him for a few days and then he would be waiting outside the factory, and I'd follow him. Weeks later he killed again, another child, another boy, while I watched.

The killings continued. After each I would go home, sweep the floor, then sit on the bed and imagine that I was the beast. It amazed me at first that I'd witnessed murders and told no one, done nothing, only climbed the stairs to my room. The corridor was always clean but for a scattering of sand, a smudged pattern by the crack of light. I'd sweep up the sand with a brush then close the door and lock myself inside. Between the bed pushed against the wall and the low window was a square of floor shining in the last sun. I'd shake the dustpan. The grains always fell through darkness into a shaft of light.

I gave up going to work. Instead I went to the library to study medical volumes, the cortex, the corpus callosum, functional asymmetry, trying to understand what made a human, what made a human forget. Retrograde amnesia, agnosia, Japanese internment camps, jungle warfare, kamikaze pilots, Buddhist monks who sanctified war, Hiroshima and Nagasaki, Bikini.

In a cold cement park washroom, I looked carefully into the man's eyes and his features congealed into an unreadable passion. The man shook his hair loose and rebound it with the red turban. His skin looked dusty. There was a pink tinge to the palms of his hands. "What are you?" I asked. "What thoughts do you have? What were you before?" The man washed his hands in the sink. Blood ran down the drain. Did this man know the millions of moments that had given him his world? Which moment had bound us together?

I found an old tea crate in the basement of my building. I searched and searched for Molly's ribbon and couldn't find it, so tied my hair back with a shoelace and broke up the crate and started making tiny houses of white wood. Over several nights of sawing and gluing, I built replicas of the murder sites, marking each death with a toothpick dipped in red. Holding the lipstick's crimson finger I caught a hot smell of lilacs. Country music played on the radio. In my hand-held mirror I tried to see my parents: their skin, their eyes. The song ended and the news talked about the murders, asking for information. I knew I should speak. If I spoke, they'd catch the man and the killing would end. Wasn't it my duty as a human being to speak? But they would ignore me as always. I made a memorial for each victim. The agony of the true witness, I decided, was exclusion.

Next morning I woke with the murderer, the man's naked body in bed beside me, both of us in a light sweat, all knees and elbows. His dark brown eyes were wide open. "I dreamed of a cat," he whispered. "Still alive, but white with frost. I took her in my arms."

I am nothing. I know nothing.

"Always after love comes betrayal." The man sat up, his body swathed in sheets. "Without consideration or hesitation. I know this. Now so do you."

"Who betrayed you?"

"No one. I betrayed myself."

"How?"

"I hurt myself." With a finger he drew a line from my forehead to his own. "After you're betrayed, you are lost."

Something of childhood was returning. Father, Grandmother, alive. My wife a girl, alive. "If I could, you are the one I'd kill."

The murderer shrugged. "I know."

When I pulled off the covers and saw his straight, perfect spine, all the tension went out of my body.

He quickly turned his head. "What's that noise?"

"What?"

"Listen." He stared out of the window. "It's boys. Down in the street. Let me tell you something — never mind."

We dressed and through the day sat together listening to traffic and sirens and the wind. In the evening we drank milk. The murderer sat on the bed and pulled on his shoes. He scratched his ear. I knelt by a beetle on the floor. An orange beetle crawling through the death scenes.

We didn't meet again for a long time. The murders ceased. I returned to my job. I heard reports of violent acts, but unrelated, indiscriminate. Invisible again, I no longer felt involved. One afternoon I curled up on the sidewalk, rested my cheek against my bent arm and woke inside a hospital where I found a roomful of women in blue light using machines to milk themselves. I watched and breathed along with the breathing breast pumps, then went to the furnace room to look for evidence of the blue lake. I took an egg from the pocket of my white overalls and ate it. Something about the egg always turned my heart. The shape and certainty of the shell, its strength and promise.

By night I tended the device that graded eggs and in the early morning went to the park to scatter seed for pigeons and ducks and a lone swan. I studied robins on the ground, woodpeckers in dead trees, swallows in the air. City workers digging and filling trenches. Seasons changed and sun blackened the backs of my hands. I was rain-drenched and wind-swept. My head filled with the erratic behaviour of roosters. I disobeyed the rules and fed the chickens fresh-sprouted grain and oiled their vents. I nursed sick pullets, mourned them when they died, buried them in a corner of the park.

I even fell in love with a woman. I'd been watching crows in a suburban apple tree when her tiny red sports car drove past the rows of identical houses, their windows shut with blinds and rippling with heat. She put long legs on the ground then climbed the steps of a new house to a patio, slipped off her clothes and lay down on a wooden chair in the sun. She was beautiful and full of sorrow. All those summer evenings I sat on the curb and watched that patio, until she sprang to her feet and vanished through one of the doors.

Night fell, and wasps still buzzed in flowers on the boulevard. The shaded windows glowed. The patio cement was warm underfoot. The moths at the window wanted something, something to do with life. Her cup on the arm of the chair still contained tea. Something was happening to my face. What escaped my notice seeded itself in the problem of what I wanted. I felt a breath on my neck. Some strand was trapped deep, some wiggling imperfection that connected my ancestors to the future, yet skipped me, that made me miss everything.

"Let us both be sudden," the voice hissed. "You were always confused by light. Now we're together again. I'll let you know exactly what to do."

There were two things. There were these two things, on one hand and on the other, no time between. To see only one was impossible, but to see both at once was also impossible because there was too much space between them. Two things. Something forgotten was returning, beginning with the afternoon, the woman, the red car, the empty street before she came. The two things were old, ancient, and they were all I had, all that was important. I wanted to keep them apart.

"Go on," the man whispered. "Give the door a whack."

The two were identical, each was unique, each a version of the other, outward difference an illusion, merely the result of there being two of them. "This is a woman," I said, "not a boy."

"I've seen you like this before," said the murderer. "Such a love of delay and hesitancy and solicitude." And then the two things, small differences sparking off them, spun in a place we didn't exist. "You want her, don't you?" There were two things, the remembered and the forgotten: I could try to affect one with the other, push one against the other, risk contamination. "To hell with it," said the killer. "You suppose a contingency that doesn't exist."

Out of the surrounding dark they were spinning, unattached and wobbly, alarmed by happiness. One was hungry and the other owned the first's requirements and they must be brought together and now was already lost. What to do. They were not parts of anything else; they were not interested in laws. If one was younger, the other was older. If one was male, the other was female. If one spoke, the other listened. If one was responsible, the other was guilty. One was right, the other wrong. If one led, the other followed. Outside the woman's window the moths tapped. *Early morning, a road through a misty valley, distant foghorns and a rooster.*

"It's home you're coming back to," said the murderer.
"Fuck her and let's get a son."

I took a breath and clutched my belly. It hurt. These
things were human. Loss underwrote every meeting. The
woman and my dreams were indistinguishable.

When morning came, I escaped the killer, followed the
woman in the red car to the airport, through customs, taking
care no harm came to her. Save and be saved, I thought,
and bought myself a ticket on the same flight as hers. We
boarded the plane together.

Six

Star, Goose and Robin flapped and soared over the city, dealing and holding and shooting up. Sometimes they hung, just stoned, fingertips stretched out, squinting down at the heads of VIPs. Oh, they heard music. They gave music. Chicks, they had cuticle. They had egg-piercers, milk teeth, baby fuzz, hard heads. They challenged everything that moved. Danced under toques. Rapped on corners. Birds and breath. What?

The music they made. On corners where streets came loose. Goose heard the others singing, then answered. Robin sang. Star was singing from a core of gentleness. Goose interrupted and imitated. They chorused traffic jam. Metal and glass round a yawn. Each sang, and singing heard, and hearing grew close.

"In the alley a corpse," Goose cried, "her ripped clothes folded where the head should be." By her side a fire extinguisher leaked foam. Star and Robin took his arms and dragged him away. Nothing would be the same. It began to snow and the snow to buzz and they loped through the

white buzzing. "Oh God, oh Christ," said Goose. "Oh God,
oh Christ, oh God."

"She had great tits," said Robin. "Great tits."

Star laughed.

Goose looked wild. "You're nuts. You're both fucking
nuts. Her head was gone. Where was her head? Someone
took her head off."

"We should've checked out the clothes," said Robin.

"I would've, except for Gooseliver," said Star.

"Fuck you."

"How much hormone would it take to get tits like those?"
said Robin.

"Could you do that? How would you do that?"

"Couple of operations, hormone therapy."

" I mean you don't just hack, it was clean, man."

"Upstairs, downstairs. Thirty grand would do it."

"What a rush," said Star. "I can't believe it."

"You freaks are totally, totally — "

"We're birds, man. Get yourself free. Everybody's got to
die."

Hail. It hailed, and boys and girls wandered away from
their homes and their homes gave them up. They walked
through the cemetery and shoved over stones, danced on
graves. They began to change. Changed into birds. They
transformed the city, and the island forgot its ocean. And
in this nameless city of cities, they hustled a population of
tourists too numerous to count. They recognised nothing,
none of their childhood haunts. They changed the Gorge
into a river and perched wild-eyed on its banks in hail as big

as apples, bruises their best pleasure. They remembered their wings and flew. Seabirds, they swam in rush-hour traffic; pelagic, they dove into basements; hawks, they rode on curled clouds. They were invisible, a snatch of music heard in passing. Strong, they were, and loved how strong.

Beaks pecked gently at wrists; claws tapped at waists.

Dek and Dit rented a cellar and lights and filmed them orgasm after orgasm. Flamed amazement. They were true birds, divided and burned in many places. Flamed distinctly. Met and joined in gentle ways through all the lightnings, thunderclaps, fire and cracks. Roaring. Though they were on an island and all around waves trembled, they knew none of it. They shook.

Whales blew off the coast as yellow-slickered armies closed in.

Afterward, on the street, not a soul.

After their fever came madness, and madness played out. Some trick. Next day it was the same, and the same for a week, the video whirring while Robin plunged, foaming. And Goose quit.

"Come here, son," said Dek.

Goose's hair staring green. Not hair but a helmet of spikes.

"Hell is empty," said Dek, "and all the devils are here."

Goose came back, what else could he do? and they were fresher than before.

"I have the island," said Star. And it was a bed, clean sheet in the middle of grunge.

"Son," said Dek, "do it by yourself. Cool the air with sighs."

Dit was almost passed out, her arms like wounded doll arms in all their scars. Dek was shooting from an odd angle. He said angel. His arms in this sad knot.

They stood on a gritty cement floor amid raw furry beams, and they were angels.

Then safely in harbour at midnight. The alley.

"Where's Sparrow?" said Star.

"There she's hid," said Robin.

"What's up, Spar?"

"I have left sleep. Home. My old man was this great person."

"It's past the season."

"Is there more junk? I got pains. Remember. What you promised?"

"What did I promise?" said Star.

"Liberty," said Robin.

"Who's that?" said Sparrow, starting up.

"Robin. Remember?"

"No lies. Promise?"

"No," said Star, "it's really Robin."

"I thought it was my father. I do not know what to do."

"No."

"Sir?"

"What's up, Spar?" said Robin.

"Yes. I am not free. I need it. Robin. Make a run for me, Robin. You know who's holding."

"I think so."

"Star, would you hold me?"

"C'mon, baby." Starling lay on the ground next to Sparrow. "I will do my spiriting gently."

"What shall I do, Star? What we gonna all do?"

"It shall be done."

Yellow light spilled on them from the pawnshop. They held hands and snuggled.

"You have kissed me," whispered Sparrow.

"Yeah, baby."

"Like my mom. Wild. Here and there."

"You're a sweet burden. Bow-wow, puppy. Crybaby."

"This feels so bad," said Sparrow.

"I'll tell you," said Starling. He made his eyes soft. "Listen to me. Nothing fades with us. We're birds, we're spirits, and we'll live forever. Shh." Star lifted his head. "Now I hear them."

One by one the others drifted in for the night, all the children of the city furling their wings. While owls swooped silently overhead, they went to sleep in one another's arms not knowing the danger they were in. A bird sickens and the healthy worry it. A bird dies and the living close ranks. Children snoring through a moment of life. Shaken awake.

Clean sheets every day on the studio mattress. Dek smoking in a corner, finger on the trigger. Dit can't keep still, can't stay awake. A fence of portable radiators. Dek in a rage.

"What have I done?" said Sparrow.

"Go on, son. Remember the fucking angels. Let's see your slit. Quit shaking. What's her problem?"

"I'm right where I should be, Dek. It's cool."

"She's right," said Star. "You moved the camera, Dek."

"Thou liest."

"Not."

"Thou liest."

"Not."

"Okay. You are three men. Let's get on. You are pissed off. Too bad for the chick. Men hang their selves. Star, tell them."

"I and my flock are ministers of fate," said Star. "You can't touch us. May as well kill water. Remember that."

"Okay, okay. You three get exposed. Children, your strengths."

"We hate this lower world," said Star. "The sea. This island. It's unfit to live in."

"Not forgetting," said Dek, checking the battery level, "all the creatures, son. Sure, it's worse than death, here. Only remember I own you in this isle. On your heads, kids. Nothing but lust. Clear?"

"Here I am," said Robin.

"Present," said Goose.

"I'm freezing," said Sparrow.

"Go," said Dek.

"Breathe twice, Dek," said Star, unzipping. "Do you love me?"

"Well."

"You have thoughts of pleasure."

"That's my business."

Fear. Anger. Excitement. Red hot air. Breathing, beat, kiss. Bending, beat, prick. Lift, music, cunt. Follow through.

"If your folks could see you now," said Dek.

"We left them in their filthy pools," said Robin.

"Lakes of cash," said Goose.

"So let's do the come shots," said Dek.

"Here I go," said Star.

Silver. Silver.

Roar.

"One more time. Lumber up."

"You said work should cease."

"One more time. All together now, prisoners, then back to your cells. Okay? Hold it. Okay. Now. Release."

Old tears. Winter. Strong.

"Your affections should become tender," said Star.

"I don't think so, son."

"Mine would."

"Where's the others?"

"I'll fetch them."

"Get those gumrubbers over here. The final scene. Tell them what I want."

"Snuff?"

"Yeah."

"Hey, Dek. We love you, man." Dek turned. Star stabbed him. And while Dek fell bleeding on the sheets, nothing false in his eyes now, Star glanced at Dit crashed on the couch behind the radiators. "I lie."

~

Owls. Sirens. The birds fly. There are many more each
day.

"I live now," said Star. "We live now under the blossoms.
I'm beat. Since I went crazy. It was well done."

Well done my chick. The music we made. The music they
made. The music we make.

THE ISLAND

On an afternoon in early summer you can smell the island's
breath before you get there, arbutus blossom, pine, wild
onion, and when you step ashore with your books into the
group of earlier exiles gathered by the edge of the forest, you
sniff the sulphurous fart of the vanished mother and the
earthier stink of her single offspring hiding in the swamp,
festering with leeches.

Slowly, over the years, everything is done, everything
read, and you don't know what's next. You've been shipwrecked
too long. You look for a sign. You speculate bitterly. You mislay
the boy for decades at a time.

HER SONS AND DAUGHTERS WERE GONE. She'd come to the island
long ago, she and her husband, when this was uninhabited
land, and they'd built the house with their own hands, the
first dwelling. Now the island teemed with life, but the
house was deserted.

She was unhappy as she drifted around the rooms,
looking at things. At the end of the day, as always, she walked
out along the track north to the tree line and stopped when
she heard running water. She touched the rotting boards

of the old smithy where her husband had fashioned swords and iron masks, tempering the metal in the clear water of the adjacent stream. After work he'd danced here in the clearing. He was a good dancer. She stood in the evening by the roadside, stroking the splintery wood, remembering smoke-dark days when the priest named children and bright days when terrifying sailors roamed the harbour. She used to visit the ships and greet the sailors, it seemed just a moment ago. Last night the old shrine went rolling down the road, the roof like a whale and the part with windows like a ship, accompanied by the creaking of unoiled wheels and clop of ox hooves as the cart struggled up the other side of the valley. She heard the voices of neighbours on their way home, crossing the little footbridge, calling good night to her, telling her not to catch cold.

Then all was silent, the frogs resumed singing, and she retraced her steps back to the house. The sky was full of stars. The air blossom sweet. She went inside and looked at the dirty bowls on the floor and saw, not for the first time, that she'd forgotten how to look after things.

Before sunrise next morning she marched out of the house and past her husband's grave through a storm of petals. The season not finished yet. She walked along the shore and looked at folk, but couldn't grasp what they were doing, and told herself they were fishing, and fishing, like springtime, was a season; her children were a season, her husband, too, and the shrine. The gravel beach grated beneath her feet. Beyond the point, out where the tide ran, she saw a hand rising. She felt out of sorts, as though she'd missed her own death, surely by drowning. The pain in her belly was like hunger, an ache she'd not felt before. *Where are my children?* The sun had just come up and mist hung over the water. A barge of palm trees was sailing through the strait on its way to another island; on the flat sea the oarsmen laboured; she stared at the red hull, the upright trees, their leaves held high.

Ridiculous, she said.

The music of invisible birds seemed old and worn and mechanical. My children have taken strangeness with them, she said. They've left me with bare cupboards and a mess on the counters and floors. She closed her eyes and heard — ah — the drip of water on boards. Their small coats hung to dry late at night in the little shrine so hot in winter, her children going up to light incense, ring the bell. She smelled her own childhood, her own far country, her father. Heard chanting and the roar of the fire; then she came outside to herself and the islanders fishing between the cool pines and the calm sea, this barge of palm trees, the restless shrine, the raised hand, no longer clear in what order the events of her life had happened. Her father had wanted to create paradise on his own island. He mapped its hills and ponds and named it Self-Coagulating. The water so calm and the red barge strong, the floating trees gorgeous with sun caught on the green bending swords of their leaves.

That afternoon she went over her children's deaths, and relief and shame were followed by an explosion of light, a migraine so sudden that she fell and struck her head on the mat, rolled over onto her back and looked at the grimy ceiling she'd last painted years ago, years and years ago. The sickness passed, but she lay still where she'd fallen. Wind blew camellia branches against the window. The bush would finish flowering soon. She remembered the men building the shrine. The farmer killing the owl that took the goat kids. Her eldest had hypnotised chickens. Her youngest rode to school on the back of a sheep. Every spring of her life, as long as she could remember, she'd carried out her bedding and spent at least one night in the orchard, but not this year. The island had come loose and was floating into the middle of the sea.

She wakes to emptiness, a thin buzzing between her eyes, rolls over and climbs to her feet and trots like an animal to the drinking barrel and her face in the water. Husband was a handsome man. His masks hung on the branches of trees around the smithy stream and to visit the dark workshop she had to pass these faces. He joked that she was too shy, too superstitious, too fearful. She crouched at the stream to scrub potatoes, wouldn't meet his eyes. She was thin as a reed.

She straightens up and gasps. The house around her is miraculously tidy, as if a cleansing spirit has rushed through. The lacquered bowls gleam in stacks. Chopsticks bristle in bunches tied with straw. Every knife in its place. The floor swept and oiled. Husband's finest sword hangs newly edged on the wall. Outside the window are the same woods, but the light has changed and sunshine creeps through the trees. A neighbour's bright voice chuckles and no one is there. Someone is singing overhead. She calls out. At the foot of the stairs she squints through dust motes adrift in the air and calls again.

There was no one upstairs. She drew a bath, lay down in hot water, and didn't move till the pain was as small as a star. The islanders are in trouble now, all of them. She nodded to herself. They'd need a long knotted rope and someone strong to throw it to the nearest land. They'd take turns for a thousand years and catch nothing but seawater. She giggled. The community was doomed. She washed her body, touching it carefully. Her skin was as pale as ever. It was her fault wind was blowing the island across the ocean. Hadn't she flirted with the neighbouring farmer? Every morning she'd leaned on the fence and listened to his stories and looked at his arms. When he held the dead owl wide, wingtip to wingtip, his heavy body open, she'd turned and he'd set down the bird and followed her home and stood in the doorway, blinking, sweating, and dirt got onto her fingers, her white skin. She lay in warm water. The house and the island spun slowly as they sailed east, toward the rising sun. She knew the heavy care of this house was finished. She was like a child again, waiting in the dark for her father's good night kiss.

Sweetheart?

Yes, Father.

I have something for you.

What is it?

An island. You must plant seeds and bear sons.

Starlight came in through the window, nothing else, and the stars were wheeling. A child's voice asked if she was sad. She knew. She knew that voice. As a young woman, after her first babies, she'd tied a scarf over her hair and put on wooden clogs and left the house and walked and walked through the island forests before the first rice and at every step had seen the ghosts of children. Whose child? Whose child? The stars were wheeling and the islanders slept on and she saw her dying father's eyes. Her brother, mad with grief, loosed his piebald colts in her rice fields. She brought in fuel for the foundry fire after Husband's day of work, thinking he'd not want her, this man sweating from the furnace, not want her sorrow. And she'd seen his own. He'd found out about the farmer. He waded into the stream, scrubbed till his skin flushed, and lay down on the grass. It took her half the night to ease his knotted muscles and in the flashing red as he reached out she saw a floating child and tried to swerve in his arms.

The islanders slept on and in the forests and valleys roosting birds fluffed their feathers, prowling animals circled their prey, as their home stirred gently at the mercy of wind and current.

After her bath, she dried herself and went downstairs and crouched on the mat where her husband had died, where she'd recently fallen, looking for stains and bruised fibres. She was glad he'd always been physically stronger than she. She smoothed the coarse strands with her fingers till the roughness was gone.

She'd kept having them, losing them. She bowed to the mat, apologising for the violence. For now it wasn't her children's faces or their eyes she needed, it was these rooms. These rooms needed her forgiveness. Travelling faster than light, the rooms flickered, her children's small sleeping bodies fading in and out.

We had breakfast at Norm's around three in the afternoon, bananas and candy bars. The bananas were green and the chocolate was melting. We were thinking, What a shock. We ate half the bananas and all the candy and talked about crossing the street. We talked about shoes. We felt good. Our shoes, what could you say about shoes? A wheelchair wheeled by the window, a beautiful cropped head loose as a balloon. The sky was dark blue and the sun hurt. We decided to have coffee. The place was full. We talked about what drives people, things like convenience, fear. We'd heard of this recluse who lived across town and wrote games. We remembered eating whipped-up egg whites sweet and baked over ice cream. There were donuts on one side of the table, coffee cups on the other. This was a sunny day in our lives. Sugar trailed from the donuts to the cups, sugar round the rims and slicks on the surfaces. We loved pastel sprinkles. We were tired because we'd been hunting day and night.

We clutched to our hearts small bags of fresh holes and got out on the street. We ate as we walked. We wondered how long it'd take to become a different person, how long teeth would last and could you invent yourself. We talked about filling in pitfalls. Some of us were bored or had pain from what or lack of what we couldn't remember or didn't want to. We could cut out anything with a knife. We had reason to live. We looked through a window and saw a baby being fed. We imagined chasing leaves blowing across a field. We remembered forests, some of us, and strange paths between familiar places. We talked about the recluse across town. The programmer. We'd go there, go see him, maybe. We told ourselves stories of decay and of things growing out of decay. It all played.

We were on a corner we liked and couldn't keep track. We went to the end of the block and back. Big jets were chasing across the sky and we couldn't hear ourselves. Nobody looked at us. We couldn't touch one another, only our own selves, that was true. We were saying, Who d'you think you are? We were saying, If you can't keep still, walk away.

We didn't want to help anyone. We made it so nothing changed, everything stayed the way we wanted. Pure. We clenched our teeth and talked about corruptions and total concepts.

We got back to shoes, haunted shoes. No one would pay attention. Shoes were too big or too small. We'd fall, maybe, and no one, not one of us, would check if that body still lived. It still played. Down there in the dark, under the cover we'd put over the pit. We wondered when we'd turn into something. We wouldn't stop here. If we ran no one would catch us. Some bodies were made to dance. We were skeletons with shoes. We were youth wasted on the young.

We had fine little bellies. We were down at heel. This was no place for children.

We sat on a bunch of crates and planks on buckets and some of us lay down and we passed the night sharing bottles and planning how to go about things, spending time on details. In the morning we saw stars crap out then sent someone to get information. We weren't staying where we were. If we decided to run, no one would catch us.

Nothing was wrong with us. We just couldn't feel anything. We had information people were hungry for, information about the universe. They didn't know. They hardly ever even tried.

We were walking down the block and one of us made a scoop shirt and we filled it with trash, butt ends, and grabbed handfuls and threw stuff at one another and bits of ash and leaf flew in our hair and we were laughing and choking, this dust so thick we couldn't see straight.

We played split with a knife. We combed out the dirt, combed and combed. We had to wait a while then, but not long. We were always waiting around. To have what we saw. Then we didn't want it. We were stoned and nothing ever changed but the colour of the sprinkles. We collected what was left out. We had teeth that could bite through anything. We licked at sweetness, say sherbet, fudge, jam. We chewed garbage and lived. Our lips tingled. We were dangerous then. We walked down the aisles of a superstore. We bit through what we stole and walked out empty. We bounced off cars and cracked windshields and lived. The invasion had begun. We were coming along the gully and we were savage.

We rolled down the hill and hit the wall of Norm's Donut Shop. We punched holes in the tires of cars parked in the alley. We went up the hill and skated down again. In Norm's we joked around. We waited for something to happen. Tow-truck drivers came in and gave us cigarettes. We talked about different things we'd eaten. Different ways we'd looked.

Jets in formation were flying overhead and we put hands over our ears. We had a big fight about whose hair was longest. We hustled out and raided the northside dumpsters. Down at the Gardens we were propositioned. We practised jumping off picnic tables. Sparrow lay there and didn't move. We put the body by the No Exit sign and next day it was gone.

We ran the show. We were as sweet as candy on blue days. We knew we were being watched. We stayed away from the movie basement where Dek had gone down. We saw that gas prices were going up, coffee was going up. We lost Finch. We went to the Gardens and lay under the fountain. We talked about nothing but the winter. Our minds filled with dreams of glory. No milk, no sugar, but lots of chocolate. We caught a cat in a bag. We were ugly and wanted friends. Our straps kept slipping. The wind from the west smelled like something else. We said we'd always be together. We felt connected. We snapped off young shoots and saved them. Our weapons made sense, they shone, ratcheted, whirred. We let the cat go. We attended a traffic accident. Robin got stabbed and bled and recovered. It didn't matter what we did.

We didn't know what we were doing and weren't responsible for anything. We wore stripes and big-brimmed hats. We lived in alleys and spent time in the Gardens and at Norm's. We could never make cash machines work. We hunkered down in the rain. When it got too cold to sleep we went to the Emergency. We leaned against the glass and watched it get white. We talked and talked until we had nothing to say then went to sleep.

We were affectionate and easy, slim and attractive. We were enterprising. We were lyrical and flexible and happy. We were wrapped. We were humorous, honest, intelligent, natural. We were enchanting and bubbly. We were ambitious. We were romantic. We were shaggy, energetic, considerate, lean and strong. We were curious. We were semi-chunky, hot, dirty and sassy. We were muscular. We were adventurous. We were pathological. We were changing.

We were changing. We didn't know what we meant.

We went downtown to kick teeth. We had dinner at the soup kitchen. We used up all the toilet paper. People thought we were cute. We thought we were cool. We stole all the time. We said, What is it good for? Good question. And threw it away. We felt happy.

We went in the pool with our clothes on. We were just swimming in the water and they were trying to get us out, poking with sticks. We had to kiss this stone face just at the surface for good luck. We were swimming out of the way of the sticks. We got bruised in the end. We had to leave our shoes behind. We saw a baby crawling by and we all started howling like a baby, just howling and howling. This was later, on the boulevard, when we got dry, and it felt pretty good.

We were walking out of a cold night. We'd been out again all night and we were tired and bleeding from sores. A person saw us and took one of us back toward the sinking moon. We watched what was happening. We killed the person, fed the flesh to local pigs at the petting zoo and next day collected the bones in a bag which we buried in the Gardens.

We woke up screaming.

We had to keep warm.

For hours we passed houses with faces pressed against windows. Trees bent double in the wind. We were talking about the garden of bones. We told stories. "The Child Demands a Father." "The Two Fires." "The Dream of the Magic Birds." We moved to a new place between two buildings with warm walls, middle of the block, right across the street from the programmer, right across from the pawnshop and the video shop, right between two trees where birds slept. Moon rising through the branches. This was before the crack up, everything frozen. Iced-over dumpsters. We stole sesame for the birds all winter. It seemed like we'd all promised to die, as if we all wanted to die. Some of us did. We wanted to die. We didn't know what to believe in or how to fight for it. We didn't want to live. We began to die. First our beauty died. We watched the birds fly up in the afternoons, earlier and earlier. Some days they didn't bother to fly out at all. They perched up there and fluffed their feathers and down below we worried about being left alone. We put our backs against the warm walls and felt cold to the bone and talked about how this would pass, the alley, the season, one another, the world, the universe. We closed our eyes. We said, Far out, the way the wild plains roll south into long valleys between tall mountains.

Cold broke us up. We didn't understand. We couldn't think straight. We were sensitive to cold. We weren't wearing enough clothes. We begged bus fare to the Gorge and stood on the bridge and watched the water stop. We wanted to jump. We ran to get warm. It was getting late. We saw a pigeon with one leg hopping about inside the fence around a construction site. It was getting dark. The pigeon couldn't fly. We went out next morning to try to find the pigeon but it had gone. We'd made a mistake. We put our hands in our pockets and talked about birds, ships, trains, the moon, wild animals, storms. We were looking for weapons. We were on our way to a place we'd never been with a message for people we'd never met and the message would kill us or them. We played with knives and felt nervous. We played again and someone got hurt. No one wanted to be the pigeon.

In the Gardens they were digging up bones. We stood outside the ribbon and watched them shaking their heads. There were green shoots coming up in the alley. The Gorge got going. Some of us disappeared. Some others arrived. We went to the Emergency when we needed something. We went to the airport when we got bored. We ran away when they chased.

Nothing could stop us.

~

In summer we faded. Things seemed to roll about. Not
us. The street. We were covered with travel dust. Buildings
and people did a slight roll. We kicked a can. It rolled and
shone. The street and the Gorge and the alley all rolled up.
Our eyes rolled. We made pig sounds. We got the shakes.
We were unwashed and broken. We found a warehouse full
of brown leather shoes with brass buckles. We recognised
authority.

We relaxed. We put arms around one another's necks.
Our ribs showed. We swam in the Gorge, under the bridge.
We were so hot. We stretched out in the water. We were
nice and ready for the softness of one another. We were
good buddies. We were dependable, durable, true blue.
We looked up at everybody crossing the bridge and went
under and pretended we were drowning and getting what
we wanted. We almost seemed to have a life of our own. By
night we were cool and rattled and jumpy. Our navels were
deep. We could cut out anything with a knife, yet couldn't
touch one another. We felt everything and it wasn't enough.
People seemed breezy, asking for it. We wanted the feel of
them. They looked cushiony and brushed and shiny. They
looked like soft takes. We were shaking so hard we couldn't
move. We had no heft, no substance, no finish. They were
fluid. We hid. We were so light they blew us away. They were
generous. They lived in colour. Our brown shoes weren't
enough. We made welts on their skin with our knives. We
were in a sweat. We were anxious. We were invisible. We

picked them up. They let us. We cut vents in their clothes. We were smoke. They didn't feel a thing. We eased into them. They were firm. We finished them off. They were surprised. For a second we were soft, gentle, lush. Almost delicate. And they were strong, with an edge. We looked through the torn cloth at the shape of the welts.

Thistle heads exploded in the alley and we couldn't stop sneezing. We held our future. Nights were short. Our faces were ugly and familiar and all wrong.

We held our shit for days, then held our piss for hours, and drank a lot of coffee. It was full moon. We went out to the golf course and crouched around one of the holes. Everything was blue. The sky came at us. We'd never felt so empty. We talked about climbing onto roofs and lifting tiles and reaching into houses and ripping out wires and starting the big fire. We talked about digging a deep long tunnel where we could live underground. We talked about stealing a train and filling a coach with dirt and having a garden with fruit trees. We talked about knife fights in arenas in front of big crowds. We wanted to be caught and held. We wanted to die. We wanted to tear out throats. We wanted to hide away. We loved the people around us and wanted to attract their attention. We wanted to kill them and drink their blood and become them. We wanted to protect them. We wanted the skin of our bodies, the skin of our bodies, the skin of our bodies. We said, If you think you are, you're not. We said, If you think you do, you don't. We said, It doesn't work backwards. We said, We are the same person. We said, This is now.

We hunted.

We were looking for the end of the gully. The gully was an alley in the gut. An opening in skin. Knives would cut through. We wanted what was on the other side. True heart. We called bullet holes false navels. We counted the generations. We got lost in how many it had taken to make us. We got lost in the stars. The lights went out. We counted so many we got dizzy. We said the buck stops here. We said we didn't feel a thing. We said it's crazy up here, back in time, deeper and deeper, fewer and fewer, more and more.

In the alley green ferns broke the dirt we thought was cement. We thought, What a shock.

We went into the Emergency with our hats on backward. We took turns in the wheelchairs. We waited in the waiting room and watched TV. People were crying on the phone. We booted the vending machines and got stuff we didn't like. The donuts were stale. Security threw us out. We watched the rain. We stood in the bus shelter and watched the rain. Ambulances kept arriving and unloading. They kept mopping up the blood. We had blades. We wanted to stay in the dark and play with the switches. We wanted to get caught and escape. We made bombs out of pipes and fireworks and bottles and gas and rags. We hid everything and collected more. At night we ran and ran. We were conspicuous and crazy and mumbled so no one knew what we meant. Jets were chasing across the sky. We closed our eyes and waited. We kept on talking, running in the dark, playing. We had

nothing but plans. The worst winter. The best chocolate
éclairs. We went to a zoo and ate ice cream. We had a fever
and slept for a week. We got sick and died. We chewed pills
and got pierced. We were a freak show. A TV crew followed
us around.

They asked us all kinds of questions. We told them
what had happened to us, the truth. The sky came at us in
waves. We'd never felt so good. They asked did we know
what country we were in. We gave them some information,
a taste. They asked what country we'd like to be in. We gave
them all our information, opened ourselves up. We waited
to see what they'd do. What they'd offer of themselves in
return. We had nothing left except this wait and it didn't last
long. They said we'd fallen through the cracks. We were lost.
We were losers. We were victims, the final victims. They
told us what country we were in. We showed our bellies. We
showed our blades.

They showed us the movie and we couldn't believe how
cool we were. Savages. It all played. Unbelievable, the way
we moved. Our eyes shone. What could this world offer
us? We'd been sold down the river and forgotten. We'd run
away and ruined ourselves. We'd inherited a generation's
loneliness. We were heroes. We were stars. In the movie
our faces were dirty. At the end the sun went down and we
shuffled around in the dust of the alley. Coloured bits of
light made a line across the screen and music started to play.
We looked small. Brave. Everlasting.

We torched Norm's and got out of the city. In the suburbs
church bells were ringing. The weather turned cold.

Everything got quiet. Anything that happened happened in front of us instead of down the block, across the street. We felt uneasy. We had to do something. Nobody was home. Things kept going off by themselves. Alarms, sprinklers, lights, doors. What we had to do was get back downtown. We couldn't go back. This time time was waiting, not us. There were no stores. The lawns were empty and green. We whispered about what was to talk about. We broke some windows, took a couple of things we didn't recognise. We'd made a mistake. We couldn't find the church. We couldn't find a bus. There were no blocks. Streets went in circles. We tossed the stuff we'd taken. We felt stupid. Everything looked the same.

We found a shopping mall. People were going in, coming out. We talked to them. They gave us money. We used the phone. We talked to the operators. We went inside and looked at birds and fish and animals in tanks and cages. We pretended to listen to people playing music. We put the money in a hat. We were afraid. For the first time, we were afraid. We looked for a dark corner. There was a crowd by one door. We hung around and looked at earrings and teeth. We were last in line for what we didn't know. We greeted one another like old friends. We played with our nipple rings and compared tattoos. We said, How's tricks. When we saw someone we wanted we looked the other way. We had side vision. We had bodies and felt dizzy. We didn't look at what we wanted. We didn't want anything. We didn't want to go in. We didn't want to stay. We didn't want to go on. We couldn't go back downtown. Everyone was staring at us.

We looked out of the glass doors at cars parked between the painted lines. The road out of there was long and straight. It went into the country, into the wild. We talked till all we could hear was wind. All we could hear was wind. Everyone here was our enemy. The road was long and straight and lonely. It disappeared in storms and forests. A piece of garbage blew down the middle. We didn't like any of it. What we'd do was stick out our thumbs and show our bellies. We'd get a ride. We'd get a ride.

Wild mint and juniper and thyme and sage, loosestrife and lupin and Turk's head lily, for the working out of harmonious dreams.

From on top of the highest hill you see the edge of the island ripple, lapped by blue. As you watch, the land changes, escapes a cloud's shadow. Alone in a vastness of sea, gulls singing the boundaries, the island looks intensely green. Overhead a jet is flying at a ridiculous speed and height above the ocean, and if you could go on like this forever, on this summer's calm day, never stop living your life, you would.

HE FLED THE ISLAND OF HIS birth, but returned in his prime to be closer to God and to marry an island woman. "Wanting is a sin," he told his wife after the birth of their third daughter, "unless it is wanting God."

"If we had a son I'd call him Ross," his wife said.

The magnolias were in bloom, and they stood under the big trees in the middle of a windy day. By this time the island was adrift, far from land.

"Ross?" he said.

"Ross," she said. "Like albatross. Those birds sailors follow."

"Wanting a son we can't have is a sin," he said. "Our family is real and what's real needs a roof. The rest is up to God."

He never spoke of his life away from the island; when asked he would grow moody, or fly into a rage until, over the years, he grew dreamy, satisfied he'd want nothing more than this, this home and family, and to see to their needs. At night, as his wife slept beside him, he considered the ways a world could change. And as he thought about the birds and the trees, the island that supported them, and felt how fragile everything was, how an island might be swallowed by a single wave, everything did change. His girls, his wife, grew old and vanished. This, he explained to himself, was one of God's experiments, one island among many, each with its memories and dreams. Any island could disintegrate, its plants and creatures become extinct. He was an old man, peaceful in his ways, and alone in the flower-quilted field, lying on flattened grass, watching tall seed heads bouncing in the breeze. Once they'd grown canola here, and field corn. Seabirds drifted overhead, pale against the deep blue sky, and insects buzzed. He rested while a heron wheeled through evening till evening was gone. He moved his arm and watched his fingers trace the Milky Way. The moon rose and dew soaked his back. He remembered the red dog he'd raised from puppyhood to old age who knew this field, these woods. He no longer needed to work his father's smithy or keep meal times or write poems. Owls called across the valley. In the distance he heard the murmur of the stream. The island must be close to land. Ferries had been seen on the horizon, and the islanders had put away their candles and oil. He didn't mind. He'd been losing weight, losing his flesh, and could hardly hold himself upright. This adventure would make little difference to him. A message from God for those who could read such things. How festive were the early years of his marriage when the island was lost. Every day, together with the other islanders, he and his wife had walked down to the beaches to scan the horizon. They'd gathered in the evenings to discuss weather and the currents that beat them south, southeast. They'd danced when they saw lights in the distance and when they crossed the equator. He hoped they'd drift again northwest so his grave would be in Japan, although his favourite daughter lived in a mainland city in the direction they were drifting. This middle daughter was proud, like her sisters and her mother, but unlike them was slender, unmarried, unsettled, and had only one child, a boy, a white-haired boy. When she was young he'd taken her to the cherry festival where she'd watched him lose at gambling. That little girl in her short dress had seen him, seen right through him. They'd been gentle girls: skin like the petals of a fresh magnolia flower. His wife had beautiful skin. His girls had beautiful skin.

As he lay on his back under the stars, his wife came in a dream, and even though his clothes were soaking and he couldn't stop trembling, he blinked awake, sighing with happiness. The summer meadow at dawn was completely still beneath frail and scudding clouds. Plans were in place to divide the island with paved streets and build a school and establish an interim council to deal with issues of nationality. Islanders had raised money to haul the shrine back to its old location. Life was simple. Today he'd pray to each grain of sand: one of remorse, one of anger, one of sadness, one of joy. He'd made his wife happy, even though he hadn't given her a son. At the end he'd stood over her and couldn't talk and she couldn't move and the doctors were coming and the phone rang and rang and the blue hyacinth was in bloom and he'd held onto her hand, remembering his grandfather's death, his uncle's horses splashing in the rice paddies, while the girls waited outside in their new white kimonos.

He stepped shivering back to the house, thanking God for this miraculous life. He stood at the threshold, morning birds at his back, and remembered running downhill to this house as darkness fell, to be with his wife and girls, and then lying flat on his back in the orchard, exhausted, waiting for supper, listening to the island's evening sounds.

He's furious today, furious at the big sky with its wispy clouds, at the immense mainland to the east, the day like an empty bucket. This is not where he wants to be, on the wrong side of the ocean.

He squats under the oak near the red dog's grave and fixes mean eyes on the row of magnolias his grandfather planted along the smithy stream, taking from his hemp sack the half-finished sandals, dabbling his fingers in straw dust. Hadn't he taught his daughters the eternal God, the certainty of land and loss, the uncertainty of water? Once his middle daughter got stuck in the branches of this tree and her crying had enraged him and he'd had to clamber up to get her, their two faces close together as he climbed down with her in his arms. Here is where he meets his family, under the oak. Prayer is full of lost children, he tells himself. They rain from heaven, no matter what country you're in, noisy in their games. He reaches for another straw and pauses. That day, when he'd set his child on her feet, she'd continued to play, ignoring his anger and her own fear. He'll send for this daughter, after all, and she will bring her white-haired son and they'll work the land. Islands can separate from the seabed and navigate oceans. Out here with the Pacific at his back ancestors surround him, the straw sandals come together, and there's joy in the tangle of coloured laces. Life is made of spinning, not a child's game, but played by children who have already vanished. He tells himself. And gathers his sandals. And goes inside the empty house. He doesn't miss them. He tells himself. He turns to look at the swaying meadow.

In the wild country we couldn't sleep. We couldn't think straight. We talked night and day. Every place was deserted and lonely. There were hillsides and trees and passing animals. Nothing travelled in a straight line. Rivers came and went. The paths were tricky. We danced on rocks and made a lot of noise. We ate berries. We came upon savage things. Climbed into ravines and got stuck and the world was ending. These were our last breaths sending out last bits of air. Counting was a funny thing to do. At the top of a cliff rain pricked our skin. We saw in the distance a lonelier place, long and grey and flat. It went on forever. It was the last thing in the world and it worked. We punched one another. Skin was the last thing about us and it didn't work. Our first thing was a sheen, a glow. A great nothingness in our lives because we would never be anything, because we would die, and knew it. We did what we could, drank rain, ate an egg, had a sleep, moaned for a while, sang a song. We got off on the view, but it exhausted us. We'd had enough.

We returned low and mournful to the city, to the laughter of kids playing, to dogs barking.

We found the city deeper, the same but darker. Dit was a nobody hustler. The alley was the same, maybe smaller. Our thoughts were blue and reckless. We rubbed knuckles into dry sockets, squinted against the glare. We remembered one another, that we needed to do nothing we didn't want to. We skidded into the intersection on skateboards.

One of us was hit by a car. The driver jumped out. The driver limped to the sidewalk. The red pool steamed in the afternoon. We put our fingers in, then hid our hands. We jimmied the glove box and stole papers and a gun. An alarm went off and the pool on the road began to fade. The driver came toward us and said, Hey! We pointed the gun and he gave us his wallet.

Okay! He backed away. It's okay!

It wasn't okay. We scanned the street. No difference between his blood and ours except Robin had died.

We opened Robin's mouth to see what was there, and the body lost its air and sank in our arms. Everything seemed to tilt. We couldn't keep still, couldn't stop working our bones, flashing on possibility. We put down the body, breathed on the open eyes, removed the wet coat. Some of us went to the park to find flowers and came back empty-handed. Our voices sounded stupid. Two dogs met at the corpse, their hackles raised. We chased them off then carried the body away. Trees were turning red along the boulevard. We'd bury this bird in the park where it would feed next year's flowers. Spit dribbled from our mouths as we dug. We expected cops to appear in the garden. The poor head rested in its grave, sky in the open eyes.

We floated around the alley. We kept going back to the park. We went to the park and stared at the brown grass trying to remember what we needed flowers for. A little girl was lifting her T-shirt to let a boy touch her belly. The mother asked the girl if she wanted an ice cream.

Uh huh.

The boy tickled her and ran away down the holly path. The mother went to the ice cream wagon. We grabbed that girl. She stopped screaming after a block. We gave her a cigarette and took her to the dump and sat in the shade at the bottom of a hill of garbage. I want my ice cream, she said. We had to make a decision. Night was falling. We were nervous. We talked about killing the girl. We were afraid of nothing. We were liars. We hated brushing dirt off a dead face. We talked about all that. On the surface we were cool. We examined her navel, comparing hers to ours.

It got late and we made a fire and gave her a sweater because she was cold. We said stay right there, don't move, and went down the road and broke into a corner grocery for ice cream. On the way back we played kick the can and thought ransom but didn't know how much. The ice cream set our teeth on edge. We sucked our lips. We hated money. We had to figure out what we wanted, what we wanted most. We put our hands in our pockets. We stopped playing. This wasn't a game. We lifted the can with our toes, tossed it high. We pushed one another, leaned hard. Went back to the dump, gave the kid an ice cream and let her go.

~

We paused in the middle of breaking into someplace and listened to people doing stuff in their rooms. We opened drapes and stared at the steeples, all those churches down in the city. Our eyes followed the streetlights leading to dark. We didn't take a thing. Being there was enough. We found an empty house with a huge pool. We were in the tiled swimming pool, in warm water, watching ourselves on TV, but it didn't work. The pool was dumb. We put all the furniture in, all the potted trees. The pots sank. Most of the trees stayed in the pots, some floated out. We smoked Dit's crack and saw the leaves turn into birds. The birds flew away in the shape of a tree. Down in the water the pattern of the sofas and chairs was the way the birds flew. It was like a swamp, everything rippling.

We met a salesgirl in the airport flower booth. She had the whitest most translucent skin. We put our arms round her shoulders. We were in the passenger lounge pretending to wait, keeping an eye on the flower girl, high on speed and acid and ecstasy. When strangers came toward us we slipped from our seats and held onto one another. The distances between our bodies kept unfolding and folding like breathing. A woman fell to the floor and airport cops moved in to hustle us out. When things got quiet, we went back inside, into the flower booth. She smiled. The flower girl. She gave us each a flower and we took them back to the alley and left them there.

On the day it never got light we hitched east. We looked up, at the area where the sun should've been, the sky. Go to your fucking grave! we called after cars that wouldn't stop. An old Pontiac with its radio blaring bounced off the curb in front of us and fishtailed all over the road and stopped. The driver was this happy dude. His wife in her red dress. In the back seat a baby. We couldn't think straight. The guy was laughing so hard, hollering for us to cram on in there. The whole day was a blur, and we slept in the holding tank all night long and got out next day because of our ages.

We were bored. We hitched back to the suburbs. We spoke to dads washing cars. Spoke to moms on their knees in the soil. Said we were collecting for homeless street kids and they gave us money and we bought booze from a bootlegger and were cooked when we got back to the alley. We slept about a week. Some baby, all by itself, crawled into our dumpster and woke us up. The child was small and had dirty hands. It believed everything we told it. After a day or two it got sick and shivery so we gave it a cell phone and left it outside a travel agency. We didn't speak to anyone for months, just smiled. There was this silence in our lives. We built a wall of beer cases. We watched TV, soaps and sports, in the video store window across the street, pretending we were heroes. Wrecked juveniles sprawling in the big easy late summer trash. We were coroners. We were detectives. We were commandos. We were workers. We were suits. The dreams and nightmares in our heads would not stay put.

Then a major score. Every morning like fog. We reached up to touch the only star we could see in the sky, laughed and laughed, then smashed all the lights, and then it was winter. No hand to break us or cover us.

After the first snow, we discovered bodies. We found the corpses of a hooker and a businessman. Coloured lights on slush like in a movie. We poked around under the broken shelter. We found dead scientists, politicians, lawyers. Found electrician's tape and a stash of needles. Wind blew in a bad smell. Sleet on the canvas roof. It was almost light when the jogger splashed by, breathing hard. She wore tights, tank top and wet runners, a yellow Walkman clipped to her belt. Her face sparkled. At the corner she did deep knee bends, rolled her head around, then got going again. Why wasn't she dead? No one stopped us, no one asked what we were doing.

We broke into the pawnshop. The woman had stopped buying our stuff. The heavy metal guitars shone. Upstairs in her apartment she was snoring and whistling, her old feet uncovered, the toes black and curled up. She opened her eyes. We were a flock of birds. She was one hundred acres of fear. We wrapped the money in a scarf, dragged her downstairs to the basement. Her head rested on a rolled carpet, the edge of her nose all torn. It was the crack of dawn so we sat down to watch traffic through the basement window and pedestrians walking by. There was a picture on the wall called *Midnight in December* with a broken fence, two rows of bare trees, a house with red shutters and lacy curtains, one lit window. Inside the room was a dog asleep in front of the fire.

We stood under the used car lot's sign that buzzed and spun slow, and listened to the programmer's voice. He said he wanted to help us, he liked us. If we did our part things could get better, otherwise it would get worse. We'd heard that before, but he wanted us to tell him games. He was going to do something, go to the government for startup money. He was going to the electronic people, the animators, the tech wizards. He'd find us jobs testing games. He'd find us a place to live. Maybe he was crazy, maybe not. Anyway, it was really cold. It was so fucking cold that we burned garbage to keep warm.

On a late summer evening rainy wind sweeps over the
island and pine needles shatter on paved roads giving off a
pungent smell; cicadas chirp; hawks leap off the world for
something they can't even call.

HOW BEAUTIFUL DUSK IS HERE. I didn't always think so, after
the farmwork, what with the quiet and the dark, this island
sinking and rising through ice ages, so tiring. I used to
think I should have stayed where I was, busy with my work
and my son, even though Father wanted me to take care of
the farm, even though he couldn't look after himself. I had
to come, I suppose. He never looked after me. I never saw
him even look at me. Every night I lay awake listening to
him snoring and often had to get up and walk and walk,
through trees dark as blood, to the end of the island where
in those days you could still see the city lights. But I couldn't
go back. I couldn't take and couldn't leave my son. Nothing
would give me the strength. I hated what I'd done. Perhaps
that's why the first trees we planted were killed by frost, and
not, as Father said, because we'd not waited for the moon.

Every day we mended fences and pruned trees and planted vegetables and Father never lifted a hand to help. His job was to steer the island, he said, but all he did was sit under the tree and make sandals. As if sandals could direct anything. We never asked a thing of him because we knew he'd say no. He praised you once, remember, that time you picked up his father's flute? He said he could see the sun shining out of you, but he never said a kind word to me. I hated his face in the evening when he drank. There was no kindness in it, no sign of love. He made you cry that time he forced a chicken to the ground and drew a line in the dirt in front of its beak. When he died ravens laughed all day long and our goats went crazy and climbed into the hills.

Be still, my beautiful fair-haired boy, and listen to that bamboo. The bamboo is taking over the old fruit trees. I want to tell you that. I want to tell you how I loved a man and you were born. Something ends and something begins. Once when I was a young girl, on a warm wet fall day like this, I climbed the oak to spy on my father through his workshop window. There he was, a pencil in his cap, cigarette between his lips, doing nothing, just staring, and I stared too, at the wind blowing the bamboo, their shadows on the white wall. Light fell on his cheek and smoke from his cigarette shivered in the air. His coat lay over the windowsill, the arm flapping. Why should I disturb him? Why was he mean to me? He didn't know I was there until I screamed and almost fell from the branch.

We danced when he died, d'you remember? We danced and broke a pillow, then danced through the feathers. Do you?

How beautiful the sky is. The sky is the same old sky. Here come our ducks. They're down here every evening when the light goes. All night they lie beneath my window, heads under their wings, and I hear them gossiping if any nocturnal creature is near the house. The world is well for me tonight. That's why I have to stay awake a bit longer, to tell you things. The world is very well. How much I loved to hear you play. You played sweetly. You played so sweetly. And I want to tell you we are moving again, the island is loose again and the wind is from the east. I will leave rice cakes on the table in case you're hungry. I'll leave three duck eggs. One for you and one each for your boys should they come. The pebbles, leaves, bones and feathers the ugly twin called warriors are in a box under the stairs.

Now it's dark beneath the trees across the field and my fingers are cold and the children are half in and half out of the forest, calling, *Mother, you shouldn't be alone, Mother, you shouldn't be alone*, their voices rising and falling. Go on. Remember Granddad's sandals hanging from the oak? A row of golden sandals in the breeze.

What kept me here? What kept me here when you were gone?

I know. I remember.

Those kids, not taunting, but calling. Those kids. They're out there now, in the nearly dark forest behind curtains of new rain and water dripping from the roof onto the house bamboo, and our ducks are sucking at the mud outside my window. Remember when we caught and killed the mink and had to bury our torn ducks? Do you? I can't tell if you're out there with them or not. It doesn't matter, I suppose, none of the children are caught or set free. But I do want to tell you one thing more: there's a fierce old demon where the door used to be.

PARADISE

WE BURNED GARBAGE TO KEEP WARM. Sleep confused us. Some were sick from bad food or the loneliness of the world. We said nothing. We were waiting for a sign. To keep warm we leapt about, pretending to shoot one another. We'd done all this before. Nothing had changed or was changing, except us. We had to think of a game. We wrapped ourselves in yellow insulation. We looked up into the night. We loved darkness. But there was old sadness under the surface of everything.

We broke into this child's room. We crawled onto the bed, lay there and watched the open door. We didn't know what else to do.

We rode buses. We got a thrill from wheels rattling across bridges. The buzz and hum. People on board seemed forgotten, left over. We were kicked out on the industrial islands. It was a cold day of low grey cloud and no news. We stopped on a bridge and watched the water below, the trash sliding under. A tall old guy and two women with a tiny baby in a stroller were walking under a tree hung with garbage bags along a path in the park. The Gorge shone from last night's spills. We broke into a warehouse and tore open crates and found little chutes and funnels that didn't fit. We skated on frozen paths and ripped down a corrugated shack in the yard of a shut-down factory.

We got to the regional library before it closed and hid in the stacks till they told us to go. On the steps we were freezing. A boy wearing a white windbreaker stood waiting for his father. We took him to an abandoned rail car. We fastened electrician's tape around his head, his lips, his arms and legs. We left him in the open freight. Searchers with flashlights entered the area. We could hear the father calling his name.

We went to a movie and twisted scarves around our arms and shared a rig. Caught sight of one another's eyes and couldn't breathe. We sat in a row, gripping the armrests. When the movie got going it felt like we were on the screen, our lives turning violent. The actors were like friends. Returning to the street was hard. We'd done all this before. Nothing was changing.

The programmer gave us consoles and a game to test. He said he was going to the bank, going to high rollers for backing. He told us to run the game a thousand times, check for bugs and crashes. It was about blood and terror, sex, whatever. He said this was our big break. He told us to forget we were kids. He said we could dream big this time. We didn't want someone to tell us what to do. It got worse.

Goose was killed. We weren't paying attention. We carried the body away. We buried Goose in the Gardens. The park was ugly. We couldn't look at one another. We felt like dying. Wheels rattled across a bridge. We didn't want to last forever. Didn't want to know it could happen. We didn't want new skateboards. We weren't sleepy. We didn't want a puppy. We were woken by nightmares. No. It wouldn't play. We sold the consoles.

The drug heated on the candle and we sat around the bed in the dealer's room. It was cold in there and dusty, underwear and socks hanging on a stick out the open window. The dealer's girl burned incense. She crept around the room, humming. She's got songs inside her head, the dealer said. When she left, he locked the door. The candle flickered on the table. All was quiet. A slight depression at the edge of the bed, the quilt rumpled where she'd been sitting. Man, he said, nodding.

We slowed to a stop each time the needle went in. Lots of cops out tonight, he said. We shifted around on the floor. He snarled at us, then smiled, closing the window a bit. Did we want credit cards? Passports? Sweat trickled down his face. He punched his fist into the wall. Told us to get lost. When he opened the door, the girl peered in. She was bright as a light. She lived in a different world.

We were bounced from McDonald's on Christmas Eve. We had no money. We tried all the parked cars. We were spooked, couldn't think of a game or an excuse to tell the programmer. We decided to walk across the Gorge to the dealer's, hoping he'd be out and the girl in. We didn't want to fuck her, not really, we didn't really want to. On the bridge a woman was trying to light a cigarette, her hands shaking, her skirt flapping in the wind. We swarmed her, kept going.

At the end of the bridge we turned. She was kneeling by the railing, throwing up. The puke swooped, catching the light, down into the Gorge. The money was not much. There were gangs working the shores, warehousemen and other, darker, shapes.

The dealer was at home and his girlfriend was in bed so Jay asked for uptown and Crow asked for downtown.

Come on, come on, the dealer whispered, blowing on his fingers, make up your minds.

We didn't really know what we were going to do. We busted in and tied him up. The girl pulled the bed covers over her. We listened to an ambulance on its way to the hospital. There was laughter, families having a party somewhere. The girl called us assholes. We asked to see her tits. It seemed crowded in the room and a long way from the door to the window. She opened her shirt. She said how stupid everything was. She had tears on her face. Her lips hardly moved. We licked her nipples. We cooked up some dope. We talked about bombs. We talked about scorching and crushing. We talked about throwing the dealer out the window. We fed him chocolate bars. While he watched we all fucked the girl. We shared one last hit, and set fire to the bed. We took her with us. We said tell us about someplace. She said there was an activist's house.

She took us there and we went in through a side window. You guys are fuckheads, she said. We said it's up to you. Under a pine tree in the corner was a pile of coloured boxes. Angels were singing. The room was like a cave. We gave the dealer's girl a present and let her go. We checked the house.

The kids were asleep. The activist and her man in bed snoring. We grabbed presents and ornaments and bottles of booze till the room was empty as a brick, empty as love. We ran back to the alley and opened our gifts on Christmas day. We ripped boards from the window of the pawnshop and built a fire. We played with our toys. Drank wine out of glasses. Cobwebs drifted overhead in the warm draughts. We set a kitchen chair in the middle of the fire. Spiders ran along the chrome. The paint bubbled. We ate cake with thick icing. We put a doll with blonde hair on the chair and she melted. We wrapped our arms around one another and lit our pipes with blobs of burning plastic on a stick and told stories. Homes falling as the people inside slept. Bulging plaster, cracked windows. Ghosts on an empty lot. All of a sudden the doll's hair caught fire. Then we saw a small hole in the middle of her belly and a hand poking out, pale little fingers. The hand wanted to pull someone in or pull itself out. Maybe here was a game but we couldn't figure an ending or goal.

Next morning it rained rivers. We were wedged under our boxes in the alley. We stayed like that for months. When winter ended, only half of us crawled out. The sun shone. Buses and trains were leaving on time. Planes were on the runway. Cars were where they'd always been.

The dealer's girl was all cleaned up, dressed in a suit. She picked one of us out of the line up. No loss. One Magpie less in the sky. We peeled jackets then sweaters, down to T-shirts and cutoffs. Arranged ourselves on corners and closed our eyes. Our skin was still perfect. Men, horrified by our skinny bodies, followed us, paid us, grabbed our crotches. We were consumed. They nearly fainted for us. We were the ones they wanted in their air-conditioned spaces. Their hands full of photos. We were babies. They went into convulsions.

Our numbers were growing. One child would vanish and two take its place. We roamed the suburbs for recruits.

Look at us, we're blocking the way.

The fathers retreated to their wives and houses and businesses. They had it memorised.

The days darkened under smoke from factories out on the industrial islands. The programmer forgave us for losing the consoles but every game we pitched him was wrong. He shook his head and said we weren't trying hard enough. We ate donuts but couldn't taste the sweetness. The touch of an adult's hand could still change everything. We were still boys and girls. We were still beautiful.

Summers we went to the wild country but it had changed. On the high cliff our faces streamed with rain, but the long view didn't work. We sat in the dark at the edge of the forest and stared out past the headlights on the highway. We listened to hissing rubber. Smelled the acid smell of cars. We blinked, then slept. Once upon a time a child asked her dad if his uniform was green so he could hide in trees. Once upon a time a father set his house on fire with a cigarette and gasoline. Once upon a time a father died in a superstore, his corpse under the lights soft with tiny hairs. In the dark we opened our eyes. We took a fresh look at all the distant things. Those stars up there were bigger than buildings. We sat at the edge of the forest. An ordinary night turned into an ordinary day. We shared a cigarette and smiled at the empty skies. Everyone got up and sat down. We were so restless. We wondered whether it meant a change in the way we felt about people. We remembered our mothers. We took turns jumping on a tree, trying to break the branches. We remembered sisters on ice, no-use brothers. We remembered home.

We were on a crowded subway, everyone sleeping or reading, and we rolled into the commuters. A woman said into her phone, It's me.

At the superstore we wandered the aisles and watched babies in their carts. The wheels squeaked. Music buzzed like bees. We wiped out a pyramid of baked beans. A door banged, somewhere back of the meat section. We took a baby. You're with us now, we told the child. We cut our fingers and mixed the blood, burned a spoon over a candle, shot one another up. We named the baby Lark. We sat facing the video store window where dummies on circular chairs looked at each other, not at the TV between them. Rainbow patterns glinted on the sidewalk. We shivered from the drug. Lark would not stop crying. A fat woman stopped to see what was happening. Get a life. Our fingers ached in our fists.

We slumped against the mesh. In the night fences had been built across the mouths of the alley and we were inside, in a cage. We hid Lark. We lay there and people came to see us. We watched them through the bars. They were flabby and stupid. We gritted our teeth. The breeze felt okay. Real summer had come and a hydrant was spraying the air. The news came and recorded our bruises and wet faces. The bars were something final we'd earned. We spread our arms. Lark lay there. We were black and white angels.

They took Lark and held us in a wing of the abandoned hospital. The programmer came to visit. He knew our bird names. It was tough to be with someone who could tell us apart. The whole evening he talked. Systems were means of exclusion. To keep out what's not wanted, what's undesirable, morally and socially. A cage is a system to exclude wildness. A hospital excludes the healthy. But we couldn't sit still.

The programmer laughed. "Here are four kinds of death. Murder, suicide, sickness, and accident. Then there's a fifth kind. The death of the master." Ash fell from his cigarette. We looked at his eyes. They blinked. "Of course," he said, "no one wants anyone to die."

We stayed by the window looking at the willows on the banks of the Gorge. Paint peeled from the ceiling and there were guards at the doors. In the afternoons the programmer came. He said we were a mess, our beds were a mess. We lacked characters. We lacked a plot. We lacked a plan. He said we were a disappointment. We said who knew about beds? He gave us one last chance. And suddenly we could concentrate like never before. We made the beds and swept the ward. There was a character called Dad and one called Mom. The trick was to keep Dad ignorant and supplied with beer and keep Mom always in a different room. What kept the game up and running kept the parts of our lives from flying apart. The programmer said, "Wow. I don't know.

Who's the hero?" He walked down the corridor breathing deeply.

We began to think up sons and daughters. But right away something wasn't right. Some glitch. Mom was dead; Dad was crashing into walls. The little dudes were fading away. We stood by the east windows in the morning sun. We kept trying to fix things. The programmer never returned. That's okay. We understood about time.

At night we could smell the Gorge. We shut our eyes. Families slept in our dreams. We loved hard surfaces. Shiny leaves. We liked architecture. We discovered marks we'd forgotten we'd made. Everything played. We were heroes getting dressed up to kill. We used each other. Everything was sex. Every moment was a movie. Other people were like us, of course. We'd seen them, alone and hungry, kind of wearing their bones on the outside. Yeah, in those days the few of us left wore pyjamas and dreamed up cool games.

On the island you are alone, you exist, but vanishingly. You need to find the essential, remove the rest. Shipwreck the beginning, rescue the end. You washed up on the strange and it became familiar; what's in front of you is unrecognisable. Be at pains to see the island as fixed and you won't forget who you are. By memory try to control the future for your child who has no history.

The story loses its moorings. The island is full of noises. Snow buries everything.

THE OLD MAN PUTS MILK IN the bottom of a cup, pours in coffee. He rushes from task to task about the house, building a fire, collecting wood, cooking bean stew, trying to remember whether his sons grew up or not. Perhaps he'll take the rowboat out and search the coast, or hunt through the abandoned farmhouses. He stops and stares at the pictures on the wall of an ugly and a pretty child, and pours himself a glass of last summer's cider and wanders, sipping, into the hallway where there's a cold draft. Not the bedroom. He'll sleep by the fire.

He finds a cup of cold coffee on the floor, sets the half-finished cider beside it and swallows a burn of whisky from his flask. He used to take his sons to fish trout in the high lake when his mother was alive. They set out at dawn, the three of them, and as morning sun touched the green haze of alder and fog drifted on the water, they rowed out, and when they'd caught enough would return to shore where the beautiful boy — younger by a minute — would climb the smooth trunk of an arbutus while his brother scowled in the reeds. Then came a time when they caught nothing year after year because there was nothing left to catch. He likes to imagine fish in the lake again, almost still under the ice, a flicker among weeds. He swallows another shot of whisky, stirs the cold coffee with a finger and lifts out the pale milk skin. One boy sickened and the other thrived. He sits that way, in chill light from the window, licking his finger.

He walks the frozen country road, the grass short and frosty down the middle, his eyes smarting in the brightness, trembling with cold, waiting for a thing to warm him, that girl like a tall sunflower holding a man's decapitated head, something still alive in the head's eyes. Where did he see a thing like that? The way her small fingers sank into the man's curly hair, so much turbulence in the background. The war. He has no other idea.

That afternoon while he's clearing his grandfather's ruined workshop of old timbers and broken things, something catches his eye and he sees on the grey window ledge of the only standing wall a ring-necked pheasant staring in at him, vivid against the churning flakes.

He wakes up next morning to a spice from childhood,
pain in his left arm, his right leg, adds wood to the fire and
makes coffee. It has snowed more in the night. He sits at the
table with his mug and takes a deep breath and lets the air
out slowly. He'll cut his hair, shave, find a clean shirt. He
puts on his winter coat and sits back down with the useless
ferry schedule in front of him. One was all grace and the
other all stumble. His love for them was not enough and
theirs for him was spoiled by growing up, and their love for
each other was a kind of hatred. He hears birds and falls
asleep a moment.

In his dreams are the usual glimpses of children killing
children. He wakes to the view of snow-heavy bamboo
outside every window aware that he'll never again sleep
against a warm body. Astonishing. He sips whisky at the table
and stares out at the expanse of white. Truly astonishing.
He never knew his father. He can barely remember the city
where he was born, but he loved his mother and the wild
games they played together on this farm and in these hills
and on the beaches. It saddened him that his wife would not
leave her city home. She said she did not trust the island.
Watched by his sons, he tossed a line across the lake. A lake
is water contained by earth. An island is earth contained
by water. What does it mean? He shakes his head. A fish
struggled in his fingers, too small to keep, and he tried to
remove the hook quickly, not wanting to leave a wound. He
tosses back the tumbler of whisky then picks up his flute
and blows into the mouthpiece and across the valley they
emerge, as always, from the line of trees, the children,
some in red, some in white, their feet rising and falling,

their mouths open, children who have travelled far, their clothes faded and heavy. One note and he's already out of breath, his life as a flute player done. His mother loved this island, loved the farm and her ducks and chickens, and he no longer resents her for sending him away to school, to a city filled with people, to meet the woman who became his wife, to tread the edge of the minefield. His mother's vision transformed his world, just as his transformed at least one son's life. He remembers the first grass growing on his wife's city grave, Albatross, the son his grandmother wanted, child soldiers bleeding into thin soil, and the summer day his grandfather gave him straw sandals with blue laces. You are never who you think you are; the selfishness you nourish in your children has in it something you never allowed yourself.

The world changes at the speed of light and his jaw drops open. When he looks down, he finds he has drooled on the table.

The snow falls for so long that it covers the beehives and the graves and fences, the lower windows and the woodshed and the duck house, the car and the power lines, all but the top of the oak tree. The day it stops is fine and the old man digs his way outside to find the sky full of light, brilliance everywhere, and he perches all afternoon on a tongue of ice by the shore to watch ospreys fly over the water. Mist lies on the waves, the tide creeps in, gulls shriek above the swells, and his mouth tastes bitter, like bones in the graveyard. He hears a warning bell and sees children spinning, a constellation of spinning children … and it's gone, the way he has always found his vest's lapel, known before his arm moved how his fingers would touch the zipper and find the warm flask. His pain is gone, too. Amazing. Old friends, these buried woods and rock, that sea, this island held by a thread to its mainland, and he feels his sons' arms clasped around his neck, spirits substantiated, and there are fireworks in the island's wake, fireworks ahead, and he does not know what else to wait for.

HOME
HOME HOME
HOME

SEVEN

SHE SAT BY A WINDOW WHILE the man took the middle seat
and between them was a slender alien spirit that neither
acknowledged. The oval plastic portholes bright. Life
swirling round them. She let her arm touch his. North
Africa is simple. No friends, no consolation or advice, no
siblings. Just the desert, the rubble-strewn plain at the
bottom of everything, before before and after after, a kind
of sex this side of terror. On the plane people laugh, wait
for food. The ghost nudges her awake and she presses her
forehead against the porthole, clouds fill her eyes, the size
and depth of them cataclysmic, buoying her. She sips her
scotch. Now she's ready to step from the wings into the light.
All to be well.

They unfasten their seat belts in a trance.

"I need another drink." She waves to the flight attendant.
"Get his attention, would you? For God's sake."

"I'm sorry."

She nods. The plastic boxes on the trays slide as the plane dips. *There will be turbulence.* She taps a nail at the window. The steward hands out little blankets and pillows. On the TV screen a storm rocks a small boat. She smoothes the blanket across their laps. The man says: "I think I will have a drink."

"I know," she says. "I know. There's little islands down there. There's lights." Under rolling credits a stocky blue-eyed boy runs on a beach under rising waves.

The hotel was close to the river. A putrid river from the smell of it, cloying and green, she imagined, like a sluggish snake. Their room was on the eighth floor and they sat on the bed and sipped sweet yellow liqueur and every few minutes she giggled and leaned across him to see out of the window. "Jesus, look at that!" She found Bach on the bedside radio and curled up and dozed.

When she woke, she looked at him. "Your breathing is strange," she said. "Are you all right?"

He opened his eyes. "I am tired. I'm hot. You look like a child when you sleep."

She refilled her glass. She took off her clothes and told him he was old enough to be her father. He loosened his collar, turned down the radio. "That horrible smell," she said. "It's like secret violence, it's the smell of drowning." She plucked at his fingers, slipped them onto her slick breast. Good. Right. "I feel okay." A little air around her for the first time. "Yes," she said. "It's fine."

~

In the morning, she clipped back her hair. Lifted the phone and returned it to its cradle. Dressed and walked down to the dining room and took a table in view of the dull gliding water where she ordered bread and coffee and a small whisky. Across the river, simmering in heat and dust, was a tract of huts and lean-tos joined by lines of gaudy flapping cloth. Her body gave a shudder. She felt a spinning. God. She was going to be sick. Westbound traffic on the airport road disappeared, car by car, behind a cluster of palms. Then he was at her side, his hand on her shoulder. Not a gentle touch, not affectionate, but not possessive either. She felt better when he sat down. He looked small and rumpled and nervous as he slipped off his jacket. Sweat marks under his arms. His thin black hair barely covering his scalp.

In the lobby sand blew through a broken window. Cleaners were busy sweeping it up, the sand, the shards. He squinted at her and said he was going upriver. They looked outside: the planet surface was joining the air. The tags on his bag fluttered. His trousers hung sadly. Glaziers arrived with a panel of glass, two men outstretched.

"You are late already," the clerk told them.

He picked up his suitcase and she followed him to the small rental car beside the glazier's van. The sun was high in the sky, very hot. Her makeup was running. Dirt along the hem of her dress smudged like soot when she tried to brush it away. "I want to come," she said.

"Get your luggage." He opened the car door.

"You'll wait?"

He shrugged.

As they followed the river along the highway between lines of palms and past yet another shantytown, she put her hand on his knee, then reached back to hunt a bottle from her luggage. "It's true. I could be your daughter."

He said, "I never minded that."

The car was the same yellow as her dress. The motor made a lot of noise. The seat felt sticky. She had a headache and to ease it she paid attention to the river, a dull brown expanse, vast as a lake, until they were overtaken by camouflaged army trucks full of soldiers. Then came trailers carrying fresh-looking artillery pieces and clunky armoured cars and battered tanks. Among these wove land cruisers driven by businessmen, the occasional gleaming Mercedes, cool women behind smoked glass. Pedestrians trudged close to the bank. Bicycle taxis zoomed beside long corrugated structures on pilings sunk in mud by the water's edge. She could see children playing underneath, in the shade, their white eyes and their teeth.

"Tell me," she said, "Where are we going?" He rolled down his window and opened his hand against the wind. The car filled with noise, fumes, and dirt. The rotten-fruit smell of their sweat made her nose prickle. He hummed, smiling a little. She rubbed her eyes. "It was nice last night."

After drowsy hours on the highway (dreams of her father and mother side by side, dead in their car, family the extent of the world), they entered a small city, turned into a cracked tarmac drive in front of a shabby building. White paint peeling from yellow walls. Drove through an archway painted gold long ago into a courtyard shaded by a single vast tree.

"I've never felt like this before," she said.

"No," he said.

Climbing out of the car was a simple act in the midst of a lot of things happening at once. Thin music from a low open window. Birds loud in the tree. His closed expression. A sense of failure. A sense of possibility. "The tree is beautiful," she said.

Then they ran quickly across the courtyard's dirt floor, past worms dangling on slender threads from the branches of the tree, drifting down into her hair. She shook them off. He spoke to a tall official inside the pillared entrance. She wandered across to the open window where two musicians were playing in a room empty but for the fan whirring above them. The man standing fingered a kind of bulbous clarinet and the other — male or female she couldn't tell — sat on the floor and wailed. The singer had no legs. She crouched with her back to the wall and faced the dark entrance where her lover and the official stood conversing. There were worms on the packed dirt and more were unwinding from the branches. Her jaw ached. A breeze came up and the threads billowed in the thick stink from the river. Through the peeling gold archway was mud and water much the same colour and two small boats with brown sails drifting downstream. Above the heat warp a jagged mountain range, blue and remote. The sun set and the scene went dull and the two boats, silhouettes now, drifted out of sight. Boys were dragging her luggage from the car and across the courtyard.

"Just a minute," she shouted.

"We'll stay the night," he called from the doorway. He walked over and helped her to her feet.

"This tree must be really old," she said. "I mean ancient."

"It's dark," he said. "Give me your hand."

She couldn't see the point — she was stoned, hungry, in love in a place she'd never been before, amazing high, more than booze — no point in connecting it all up. Life really swirled. They climbed in and out of bed and washed in brown water and finished a bottle of whisky and ate the food sent them. She heard a man shout the same words over and over. Other voices crackled from a radio close by, but she couldn't understand a thing. They slept and she dreamed of her parents and of children. Everyone losing one another. They had sex a thousand times and learned nothing because each time she stopped to listen, he also stopped, and at no time were they untangled or unguarded. After they heard morning prayers she knew less and less. He was out of breath and nearly unconscious. She held him tight. Grime coated their skin. Day came and a terrible headache and she started another bottle and a sign on the window said *LIFT NOT TO SEE OUT*. The fan moved as slowly as they. She trusted him only inside her. It was almost night again.

"Look, I need a walk," she said.

"I can't move," he said. "And it's dangerous."

"Don't worry. Give me fifteen minutes alone. Okay?"

She shook the flask from her bag, slipped it in her pocket, sneaked downstairs, past the man snoozing in the entranceway, and through the arch toward the river. A cluster of cement buildings with rust-blotched roofs blocked her view of the water. Gulping whisky, she plunged down an alley. She was not afraid, really, though this was crazy, what she was doing. They'd rape her, steal her money, passport, her clothes. She'd disappear. But she needed to get to the river, stand on the bank, maybe touch the water.

The buildings were more extensive than they'd first appeared. A little village resembling an army barracks contained a maze of identical alleys. The sky grew darker as lights shone out from doorways left and right. Men and women sitting in front of their dwellings tracked her, their hands idle, eyes without interest. Cooking smells and the sounds of laughter and singing filled the compound. Night prayers curved the air. She gave up the river and returned to the hotel. His new shyness and body.

"It's incredible," she said. "Sapporo, you don't want to stay cooped up in this room."

He was standing by the bed, regarding the floor at his feet.

"People live here," she said. "Come and see."

"You don't know me." He was crying, yet his body was still. "I have done terrible things."

"What?" she said. "Are you going to tell me?"

"No. I don't know. Not yet."

"There's a tavern at the bottom of the steps behind the hotel. Come on."

He would not look at her, his mouth tight closed, and just when she decided to scream, her eyelids fluttered and the hotel yielded and buildings collapsed, and she stood on a crumbling embankment. Ahead were the distant mountains, peaks pure white. She made her way down the slope to the mud plain. The ground was hard. Fine sand blew against her ankles, sifted into heat cracks. Her lover stood a little way off, his mouth now open. She could smell the water but could neither hear nor see it. Boys were gathered in small groups, their voices buzzing in the breeze from the river, and men were approaching across the dried mud. Dressed only in dungarees, they walked slowly, bare feet kicking haze at every step. They dragged a dripping net, a heavy pouch between two poles, the poles slung across their shoulders. They stopped in front of her and asked if she was a tourist. If she was lost.

"No," she said. "We have work here."

"We?" one said. They were young muscled men with cropped hair, polished faces and clear eyes. The mud on their legs had dried into a light brown mosaic. Little chunks of dirt clung to their smooth skin. They eased their load up onto a shelf of baked mud. Silver flashed inside the net, the bodies of fish, and amid the fish something large.

"What is that?" she said.

The grey shape convulsed and a pale flat face pressed against the mesh.

They glanced at one another. "We caught it swimming in the shipping lanes."

She jumped back. An encrusted beast rose amid the silver fishes.

The men had left the catch and were almost at the embankment when they turned and shouted. "It's a thing of darkness. We don't want it."

Sapporo shouted that they were tourists, not parents.

"This is a child?" she said.

He ran to her side. "This is the devil," he whispered as the net loosened and the creature shook free and trembled in a glittering cascade.

"You can make sense of it?" she asked.

"This is not a man," he said. The monster skidded to its knees in front of them. Amphibian in a husk of scales, slick and sticky, a brick for a penis. Large white birds were flying fast and low above the river. She felt embarrassed. The boys around them were conversing in low nervous voices. They moved off, the three of them, toward the maze of buildings.

The creature, dry now, quick-limbed and sly, skittered ahead of them down the tavern steps, darting a glance at her and uttering a guttural curse.

That place full of honeyed smoke. Some men were in uniform, but most wore jeans and T-shirts, and the women short cotton dresses. The fishermen made room at their table. This had been an army base, bunkers everywhere, all the buildings connected by tunnels, they'd give her a tour, if she liked, through missile silos and nightclubs.

The government was constructing modular housing in the desert where no one had ever lived, no one should live.

She said, "What are we doing here?"

Sapporo's breathing sounded laboured. "I don't know." He inclined his head, listening. "I thought— But I don't know."

"Who is this?"

"Kagura."

At the name, Kagura crouched at his side, fists clenched, luminous eyes watching her.

Glasses of beer, warm and sweet, crowded the scarred metal table. The young men told her that with every spring came the threat of flooding and the military had never completed their plans for holding back the river and at flood time these places must be evacuated. The government didn't like people living in war installations. The government only feels secure with our people out in the open.

"They want to destroy us."

"No, no. They need us."

"Your husband will not mind?"

So she danced, not choosing one or refusing any, looking into their eyes, while Sapporo sat looking dazed, and the monster kept watch under his chair. One of them put his hand on her thigh and his finger curled; she shook her head no, went back to the table.

She dreams of her mother's eyes and her father's eyes, and of someone she can't remember, and it seems deliberate, this cell with the mattress on the floor, the stink of old water. Their rough hands are purposeful. Her father loved moss, which her mother thought invasive, and between their philosophical debates he replaced their lawn with a green spongy patchwork she spent her childhood rolling over, absorbing the fragrance of earth and tiny flowers. Once she fell asleep in the middle of the moss field. Father came by starlight to lift her, so cold it hurt to get warm, her arms throbbing from holding tight to his neck.

A grid of rusty metal protects a bare bulb set into the ceiling. On a hanger suspended from the grid are her clothes. A galvanised basin in a corner above an open floor drain. Four cement walls. An iron door. Beside the door a switch. The concrete ceiling has begun to disintegrate. The mattress's blue ticking smells of sun and dust. She has slept deeply. Her senses have a childhood clarity. She listens to muffled voices, far-away music, men singing. Her fingers play with a button on the mattress, round and round, digging under to test the strength of the threads. She gazes at the bulb in its mesh. The blackness interrupted. What a relief. This light.

EIGHT

MY FATHER FELL FROM THE EDGE *where we were hiking through fog after fishing and catching nothing and slid on the scree down toward the valley past every snag and bush and handhold till he came to rest in lush grass near the river in the bottomland and when I reached him he was as small as perspective had made him from above. Tiny. The air bright and fresh smelled of sun on wet reeds and new wild roses and I held my father in the palm of my hand and birds sang and the river sang and I placed my lips over his whole face and he died and I told him I loved him.*

Crossing the sea is the hardest thing I've done even though I was made rough to endure salt wounds and clogged lungs and even the glassy calm days floating on my back. I kick my heels east to find Brother lost among unpromising and worthless rabble. I am a soldier like my father. Our ancestors were Samurai so war and secrecy and disguise and faith will suffice. Brother was born a minute after me and I am his strength and not stupid. A wave fills my eyes and sun bubbles on the horizon as I swim east along the street of sharks, snatching crumbs from their bloody jaws. Curse his restless soul. Stray winds drive the youngest son

because he's weak-willed and dumb and neglectful and ignorant.
One day I'll tear his throat out. Curse him and his son and his
son's son, an exhausting list, the future. So from Cape Erimo I
swam the Pacific to Juan de Fuca Strait. I crossed Canada on
foot. Hit the water at Trois-Rivieres and let the St Lawrence carry
me into the Cabot Strait and the Atlantic. All for him. Through the
spicy Mediterranean to be with him. Bless him. I told the boys that
killing's a way to avoid loss and telling's the way to shift fate. But
O it's a battle, the going forward and letting go.

She lay on her back. She remembered the stink of Kagura
down by the shore and the night her parents died, the car
skidding on ice, defrost on high, the whirr of the fan, snow
falling on the hood. Big dark flakes gathered on the dash
along with broken glass. Her mother's hands gripped the
wheel. Her father held the side of his face and coughed. She
would put on her clothes. She stood on the cot, unhooked
the hanger from the metal grid. The door was not locked; it
was easy to open.

She leaned against the jamb, dust in her face, daylight
crimson, ochre, green and gold. Beans and grains, fruit and
vegetables on stands. Gaunt women in threadbare shade.
Men pushed wheelbarrows under flapping awnings. She set
out into the flow, bent double by the ferocious stink of hops
and chemicals. A man called from a doorway. A cat rolled
on its back at the threshold. Inside, men grunted round two
massive vats connected by pipes topped with gauges. He
called again. She asked where was the hotel, the one with the
courtyard, the big tree? He put his arm over her shoulder,
spun her, pointed to a group of women and toddlers in a

shop across the alley. He gave her a little shove. The other men laughed.

A young woman with a pocked face flashed a smile. "Come in, come in." She was tall, slender. Thick black hair rippled over brown shoulder blades sharp as stilettos. She opened a bead curtain into a small room filled with crates. "I am Suto. These two are mine." The children were beautiful, their skin midnight velvet. They sat on a blanket and stared at her. The young mother spoke through the curtain to the women outside as she stroked each child's face. The other toddlers crowded at the door. She clapped her hands; her children rushed away. The beads crackled. All the kids shouting and dodging down the alley.

Suto said she had to drive into the desert to see a sick friend. "You come with me. I will take you to your man, your husband."

They zigzagged alleys till they came to an open area. Uniformed men with guns stood smoking at the entrance to a fenced compound. "Wait here." Suto crossed the empty square. She covered her eyes against the sun as she handed papers to the soldiers and they let her through. Shortly, the big gate opened and she drove a Jeep out. She idled the motor. "Get in! Get in!"

A minute or two later they were across the road from the hotel. The long windows flashed silver. "Well?" said Suto.

"Okay."

"You can pay me, Mira."

"I have no money."

"I think you can get some for me."

She took the stairs by twos. He lay asleep on the bed under the slow fan. No Kagura. She stood in the room and looked at her pack. Panic, a still kind of panic. Before she'd opened the door to climb out of her parents' car, she'd felt time slip and, in the certainty of their deaths, had not known where she was or what to do next. A prayer call began and she spoke his name. Then she slung the bag over her shoulder and went back to the Jeep. "I want to go with you." She held out the money. Suto folded the bills into her pocket.

The sprawl of concrete buildings gave way to orderly blocks, glass office buildings, boulevards with trees, billboards. Over the roar of the Jeep, Suto said that her children, all the children, only knew war. Even she could not remember a time of peace.

"They won't bite," said the old woman.

She was stick-thin and she sat in a shack made from salvaged wood by the river on the outskirts of the city. On shelves behind her were dull bottles. Dried herbs hung from hooks. On a plywood board in the roof's overhang dangled small animals.

Mira leaned forward. The rodents twitched. They were pinned by the tail. She stroked one drab coat. The animal gazed at her through pinkish eyes.

"It's not a rat, is it?"

The old woman laughed.

Suto ducked inside, plucked out the nail, laid the slack body in Mira's cupped hands. "Now you have to pay her."

"Does she have anything to drink? Whisky?"

"Wait in the car. I'll see. Give me money."

The rat lay still, panting, on her lap, a little dried blood on the fur round its mouth. She wasn't afraid of disease. She didn't want to be responsible for any lives, but she didn't want to say no. She stroked it with a finger. The young woman beside her gunned the Jeep along the highway beside the river.

"You have no children?"

"What?"

"No children."

"No. I have no children."

"What do you do?" Suto passed the bottle. "What d'you want to do?"

Mira tilted the bottle, burning her mouth on the liquid. "My God!"

"Drink slowly! You're not used to this."

She smiled. "I'm sick of my life. My mother and father just died. My marriage is finished. Everything."

"You don't have children. You're free. I suppose you know that?"

Warmth hitting her gut, expanding. Suto's hair flying.

"Last night I saw you. Your husband is rich?"

A billboard showed a sweating politician in white shirt and tie standing beside a drawing of what looked like a subdivision, an oasis. Mira took another drink. "I don't know anything about your country." She had to yell over the Jeep's engine.

Suto shook her head. "Four different armies now. Our tribe, our allies, our enemies, their enemies. It is complicated. Arrests, tortures, murders." She pulled the Jeep over and tied her hair back. "Prisons in the desert. They call them shelter projects. The government. They stir up border skirmishes to hide tribal wars. They pay warlords to keep the people disorganised. But we're learning. Everyday stronger. No matter how many of us they kill." She slipped into first, shifted through the gears. "There are the children."

"You're a child yourself. Are those really your children?"

"Yes."

"But you're educated."

"O yes." Suto grinned.

They flew through irrigated green fields at the river's edge. Mira tipped the bottle to her lips. Wind and sand rushed through the Jeep. A week ago sorting decades of clutter at her parents' house, dealing funerals, insurance money. Now they were in the desert. Her body, light as a feather, rode flat terrain scattered with rocks.

In a couple of hours they came to a fortified compound. "This is the prison?"

"Shelter project. Remember?"

"Your friend is here?"

"She is dying of cancer. You are a nurse."

"Won't they check?"

"They will trust the papers. They will trust the Jeep."

At the gate soldiers with machine guns examined Suto's documents and waved them into a fenced lot where they left the Jeep.

Mira dripped water on the rat's whiskers and eased it into her shirt pocket, against her breast. She followed Suto across the flat desert floor. An arrow sign over the next gate said *HOSPITAL*. Two guards greeted Suto and she said something quickly and they stared at Mira before bursting into laughter.

Inside the chain-link narrow paths connected tiny buildings like motel units, each with a single window and doorway but no door. Most contained one or two people lying on mattresses. An old man hobbled from room to room, leaning in to check the shadows, exchanging a few words then moving on. At the far side of the compound a man was yelling at a big skinny dog outside the fence. The dog barked and lunged, its two front paws weirdly loose. The man kicked dust and rocks and the dog yelped and retreated. Mira saw the glint of a stethoscope beneath his robe before he disappeared round a corner. The dog bellied under the fence and came wagging to greet them. Beyond the fence lay packed dust, nothing repeated forever, nothing divided by nothing as far as the eye could see, or almost, because in the distance were dunes. The sky milky yellow, pale blue. The dog kept jumping at them, its lame front legs collapsing every time it landed.

"This is a quarantine area," said Suto.

"Cancer's not contagious."

"Everything is contagious."

The dog barked at them and outside the camp others answered, and the barking blended with the roar of a jet. Then a rooster screamed and a bell began to ring high and sweet.

Suto stopped at a thin blanket tacked above a doorway. On the ground outside a small boy held a large egg. He glanced up through long dark lashes and asked if they knew what bird produced such an egg.

"What's your name?" said Mira. She knelt beside him. He cracked open the egg. A putrid smell huffed into the air as the soft form plopped on the dirt at their feet. The two halves of shell rolled away spraying a blue-green dust.

"A dragon," said the boy.

"It's a flamingo," said Suto. "A baby flamingo. Very bad luck. Very bad. You must bury it. Understand?"

The dog limped to the dead bird. The boy shooed it away. He poked at the bird with a stick, pinching his nostrils with his free hand. The head flopped away from the body.

"Take it away," said Suto. "Now."

They crept under the blanket into the room. The smell inside was the bird outside. But human, Mira thought. A thin grey woman with a distended belly on a faded blue mattress against one wall, her face hollow but beautiful. The eyes, huge and black, shone with life. On the wall above her a photograph of the politician beside a picture of the Virgin.

"She's pregnant," said Mira.

"This is Helfa," said Suto.

"The foreign factory blew up," said the grey woman. She held the sides of her belly.

"The cancer moves quickly when you're young," Suto said. "Faster when you're pregnant."

"I am dying." Helfa stared up at the ceiling. "There are some things I still wish to do."

The rat pushed its nose out of Mira's pocket. She picked crumbs from a bowl on a crate, softened them between her fingers. The raw mouth opened and shut on the grain, tiny claws holding on to the pocket's edge.

"My baby should not die," said Helfa.

Mira nodded to herself. For a brief second she could smell the cedar patio and pastel house in that subdivision on that other continent. For the first time she allowed the picture of her husband: her husband roaming the new house before he left. She watched the boy through the doorway. He seemed more beautiful than any child she'd ever seen. He moved in a time all his own, yet he'd seen her watching, was conscious of her attention.

"Give her your clothes," Suto said. "Take her place for one night. Tomorrow before sunrise go through the tunnel under the fence. We'll be waiting for you."

"What?"

"Pay attention. Listen to me. You can help us."

Mira looked at the woman dying. Suto was saying she hadn't the strength to go under the fence. Her baby would die here. Outside it might have a chance.

"But that's crazy," she said. "They're not stupid."

She looked round. Everything was under great stress, about to crack. A child seemed impossible anywhere. She undressed and pulled on the woman's robe and sat on the edge of the mattress. The pregnant woman put on her clothes. The jeans didn't button up, but the shirt was long and loose. "My brother is dead," Helfa whispered. "My parents are dead. The father of my child is dead." Her fingers kept darting to the shirt buttons.

Suto supported her friend to the door. They paused. "Daam will keep the nurses away," she said. "He will bring food and water. Here is your bottle." She set the alcohol on the ground. "We'll meet you tomorrow at sunrise. Listen for the Jeep."

The boy said he'd buried the dragon in the desert. He said it had powerful magic, so strong it changed a black woman into a white woman. She showed him the rat, and they righted the upturned crate and arranged a nest inside, filled the bottle lid with water, and placed the rat in its new home. All afternoon she drank and drifted in and out of dreams. The boy played quietly just beyond the doorway, the dog curled at his side. From time to time she heard footsteps on the nearest paths, but no one stopped.

She remembered the empty bottle chiming dully as it fell over.

How powerful it was, the dying woman's instinct. She looked through the doorway at heat ripples, the long plain, then mountains and valleys it would take months to cross. Yet an instant carried a person into and from life. She touched her forehead. Drank some water. That night, in the darkness, she wrapped her arms round the sleeping boy and waited for the sound of the Jeep. Stars filled the window and doorway, gently fading as dawn lit the sky. The desert black and white. She didn't mind tears flooding her eyes. Above her head, the political leader gestured at the heavens and the Virgin contemplated the floor of the narrow hut. She cupped a palm over each of the boy's round knees, tracing with a thumb the small floating bone. She woke to brilliant light and fever, sore breasts. "What time is it?"

The boy regarded her. "You are sick."

"No. No. Did the Jeep come?"

"I will find another egg, a tiger this time."

"A Jeep is supposed to be here."

"I will bring a tiger."

"Please listen to me."

"No. The Jeep did not come."

"Okay. Water, then. Whisky if you can. Okay?"

"Okay." He ran away, calling the dog.

She got up and felt dizzy. Some bird was trilling. Down in the crate, the rat's home, the rat was on its back. Kneeling, she cradled it. Still warm and pliable, eyes fogging. The boy returned with water. She drank. Then she showed him the rat and asked him to take her to where he'd buried the flamingo.

In soft sand just outside the fence, they scooped a small grave.

He had dark hair, dark eyes. His T-shirt said *COWBOY*. A small dish-shaped white scar was etched beneath his right eye. His full lips were slightly parted. He had a habit of holding one hand to his mouth and blowing quickly on his knuckles. His fingernails were ragged and dull. She followed him back to the hut, watching the natural way he allowed for the uneven ground beneath his feet, the way his body swayed side to side. She imitated his walk, felt the desert in her spine.

"That bird singing," she said, "what kind is it?"

"A bird. A singing bird."

She ate the pale lentils he brought her. Had he been far into the desert?

He pointed through the door, into the haze beyond the fence. "Very far. Very far."

"Do you have family?"

"All dead."

"The woman that was here?"

"Aunt."

"What happened?"

"We had to leave the village. The water was bad. We had to leave."

"Why was the water bad?"

"Poison."

"Poison?"

"My father was killed in the factory. A lot of people died when the factory blew up. The land is dead. I have no home. I will fight. Soon I will get my gun and I will fight." A thin whine drew her attention. She went to the door. Only a jet flying high above the desert, its trail slowly evaporating till the fuselage and trail were gone. Another jet followed the same route across the sky until this jet and its trail had also disappeared. The boy gave a moan and she turned. He shook his head. "Bad times, very bad," he said. "You should go back to your country."

"Maybe the Jeep will come tomorrow."

"There will be trouble for me if you don't go." The morning wind died and it was silent and exquisitely hot. The boy sat leaning against the wall just inside the doorframe, left leg stretched out, the other bent at the knee, fingers interlocked around the shin. His head drooped, his eyes closed. He mumbled. His chin on his chest, pink tongue moistening lips. "You will give me trouble."

She lay on the mattress. Then turned to look at the boy. "Daam?"

He didn't answer. The inside of his arm was delicate in the light. His ears looked fragile. She could see it. This unbreachable fearless perfectly poised body. She could see part of a slim thigh through the displaced knee-hole in his jeans. He'll kill people. She could see it.

"I would like to go home," she said. "Will you take me?"

He sat up straight, gazed at her. "No. I cannot. How?"

"Under the fence. Whenever you want."

He paused, then looked away from her eyes. "Okay." He raised his knuckles to his mouth, touched his upper lip. "I will take you." She listened to his quick breathing. "On foot is best. Three days to the city. We stay off the roads. We make a deal, okay? No money, but you take me to America. This is possible."

"This is not possible, Daam. Your home is here. We'll find your aunt."

They sat cross-legged on the gritty floor, facing each other. Light air rose and cooled and dropped rain and moved on. The atmosphere of the earth slipped, wind blew, the paths of plants and animals continued, and the boy crawled across to her and they lay down on the mattress. She looked at his closed eyelids, the long immaculate lashes. His knees touched her belly. His shins lay easily along her thighs, toenails rasping against the skin. Her hands found his and trapped them.

"You have children," he murmured, tucking his head beneath her chin. "You have a son."

"No," she whispered.

"Why?" he said into her throat. "For a woman to have children is easy."

"No," she said.

"You are from America."

She shook her head. "I'm from Canada. A very big place."

"Not bigger than America."

"Yes, bigger."

They slept through the second night without hearing the Jeep, and woke at dawn to the bird's sweet whistling. Her fingers were numb, her breath a parachute above the cot. The boy had curled into a tight ball against her belly; she was curved like a new moon around him. The dog, panting, blinked at them from the doorway.

NINE

MICE LIZARDS SNAKES BEETLES SPIDERS SCORPIONS hurry from owls and from me, a clump of trees in the sky, then ostriches zebras giraffes donkeys people camels. There's fresh blood on the fur around my mouth. Sun, the rocks sprout long shadows and the floor of the world is etched with black parallel lines, are you frightened or afraid of me? Brother calls, Come here, come, come here, come, and together we watch shadows and emptiness, all bitter dust sky crazy wind night hunters. He strokes my back. His smell at the end of every feeling. I look in his eyes and tremble. Children once. Both of us.

The dog loped ahead in the sand, front legs splaying, paws flopping down, strong back legs propelling her forward. Her ears flew up, eyes flashed, tongue lolled. She made spiral tracks up the long dunes and plunged down the lee sides. The boy called often and she always turned and wagged her tail. When the wind began to howl and dust snapped at their faces, she stood still, front legs buckled, and barked.

They raised the hoods of their djellabas and fastened a rope to the dog's neck. Sometimes Mira stumbled and grabbed a fistful of cloth near his shoulder and he stood and bore her weight. The wind came on. When they got to the next valley between two dunes, they stood hunched together, all three facing away from the streaming storm. It was dark now, sky gone. Sand moved like water around their knees, cutting at them, as the boy urged them part way up a dune, where they collapsed together, covering the dog with their djellabas. Wind eroded sand from under them, sand hissed against their ears, and they began to slide while stinging wind reached into their nostrils, mouths, eyes. All air dense with sand. Sand scratched their eyes. Wind screaming in the dark. They sipped water to swallow the grit. Then she's buried. Grains beneath her eyelids. She hates Africa. Her eyes are inside a monument, inside solid rock, aware of electrons.

The dog pushed its crusted nose in her hand. She threw her arms round the boy and the dog. They would die. They were tiny, solitary, and there was nothing to do.

She woke to enormous silence and lay amazed, numb with cold, thinking she was blind. She'd fallen onto her side and was supported, every bone and curve of her body, by sand. Two creatures beside her were gently breathing. Raising fingers to her face, she found brooches of hard sand where her eyes should be. She crumbled the sand, pried apart her lids, and found that the top had blown off the world, all warmth had escaped, and she was blinking up into stars. No daylight, no punishing heat, just this frigid empty vision.

Hopeless. The sand chill on the surface, warmer beneath. She counted satellites.

Midmorning they came to a plain at the end of the dunes and a village of tiny huts where women around a big tree were passing hand to hand a yellow clay bowl filled with milky liquid, each taking a sip. Daam and Mira joined them, then helped wrap the tree in blue and gold fabric. The women swayed and sang. Afterward, they spoke to the boy then came forward to talk to Mira.

"The desert advances one meter every month," said one.

"Small deserts become big deserts," said another.

"The forests are disappearing."

"This is why we must plant trees."

They pointed at small figures in the distance. Mira gazed at the pinpoints of colour blurred by heat warp and dust. A hawk cruised high above.

"There are deserts and deserts," said the oldest woman. "All getting bigger." She counted on thin black fingers as she sang out: "Mojave, Atacama-Sechura, Patagonian, Kalahari, Namib, Sahara, Arabian, Kyzyl-Kum, Takla Makan, Gobi, Gibson." She stopped and stared up at the hawk.

The other women laughed and applauded. "We are all waiting for rain to fall."

"What about the fighting?" Mira asked.

"We fight this desert," said the old woman. "This hungry desert." She shook her head, then smiled. "But we are hungry too, and it is our job to plant trees so our children can have wood for heat and cooking and shelter from the sun."

"We are more hungry," a woman echoed. "Wars are wars, but trees give us fruit and shade."

"This tree is sacred," said the boy. "It has a spirit. At my village I will show you more magic trees."

They drank from a bucket at the well, filled their water containers, ate a meal of curds and grain and dried dates, then slept through the midday heat under the tree.

Through the night they crossed a rock-strewn plain, resting every few hours, then slept next day in the shadow of a boulder and repeated this for two more days. At dawn on the third day they saw camels in the distance and followed them east to the boy's village where the caravan was resting under three vast trees. "I was made under these," Daam said. She looked up into the dusty leaves, aware of the men smoking, watching her over the backs of their resting camels.

"Where is the factory?" she asked.

He pointed west. "One hour. Nobody goes. It's a bad place."

"Do these men have drink? You know. Booze?"

"No. We will not talk to them."

The men were walking about, stretching. Then they turned away.

At night the sand lost warmth, heat rose into the black sky, and the caravan moved off. They left an old donkey staked beside the well.

"These trees," Daam said. "Their roots go to the blue lake in the middle of the world. Their leaves speak. Under these branches is a place to make strong things."

"I can hear my heart," Mira said. "I can hear my heart and taste my blood. I'm freezing."

"The trees are thirsty for light and water," the boy said. "They only have to wait."

"Wait how long?"

"For the right time. The right moment."

The wind blew across her breasts. She cupped her nipples. "I had nothing to wait for. Do you understand?"

"It's different for us. We have to defeat our enemies."

"That's right," she said. "You have to defeat your enemies."

"After I come with you. After I get rich I will come home."

"I used to think everything would be fine if I had a baby," she said. "Now I don't know."

"I'll look after you," he said. "Your husband will like me."

"No husband." Trust him, she thought, he is a child. There's no room in this desert for mistrust and that's a good thing. It will take forever for the roots of this tree to reach the middle of the earth. That lake is safe. All of us will die, the donkey, the boy, the dog, and me, and it will happen in a certain order. She felt hopelessness shift. She wanted them never to let go of one another.

TEN

BROTHER EATS WITH THE TREE-PLANTING WOMEN, one a photographer from Japan, pale Japanese, her sleek voice like falling water. At night I creep close to watch them sip water.

Beautiful mystery, she says. God once lived in these places and spoke to the tribes through their soothsayer's dreams, but no one dreams any more.

My bare fangs taste her. This is the start. My teeth will grind hers. Her skin will be mine. What's in her head will be in my head.

What is that? she asks.

An old dog, Brother says. An old dog has been following me. He's too afraid to come closer.

In the small hole I've made in the dirt what's hungry in me suddenly moves and I bite the inside of my cheek. And he steps to the edge of the firelight and brings bones to gnaw. He says, Stay. Good. And turns from me.

The camera lens is useless, she says. These planters have a sense of time and community inconceivable to our minds.

Her back looks delicious, her narrow thighs, her haunches, but I must stay.

All morning the women work, all afternoon they sleep in their tents and at dusk Brother brings scraps of an animal too long dead. Find her, he says. Find her. He scuffs the gravel in a circle and I nose across the sand to the village where Mira's scent sleeps with those of a dog and a donkey and a tender boy. There's a circle round the moon and the donkey catches me. Our nostrils twitch water, yet he is tied and I am free. After drinking I leap through shadows, rub my belly against the sand and Mira laughs aloud.

A voice had called her from sleep. She stretched out her arms. The boy, cross-legged beside her, gave her curds to eat. The dog came bounding. The awkward gait. Those turned-in paws. That evening they found flowers growing in powder-dry sand beside the well. "Are you sad?" she asked. "You seem sad."

"I need to leave this place."

"What about your aunt's baby? Who will care for her baby?"

"Yes. Yes. But I need to leave."

That night as they walked her legs felt strong again. She watched the shapes of the boy, donkey, and dog crossing the plain through scattered stones. Up above, needle holes in the sky's velvet, a faint smoke sifting through.

"Planes sprayed dust on us," said the boy. "Then soldiers took us out in a helicopter. They took the children then the others. They put yellow crystals in the well. They shot some of the men. Some girls and women and some boys, you know, the soldiers raped them." His voice on the still air. "People fell down and blood came from their eyes. Helicopters took us to the hospital shelter. Many people died."

She put her hand on his coarse black scalp. He allowed this only for a moment before moving out of reach.

"When it rains in this place there is water."

"How often does it rain?"

"Every two, three years. Sometimes not for many years." He stopped and squinted at the sky. "Those birds mean a little water now. Those birds soak their feathers then fly home so the young can drink."

As they headed toward the promise of water, first sunshine flooded them.

She could almost imagine him in a northern city surrounded by parks, highrises, foggy streets, crescents of houses. Knowing the city the way he knew this land. No. It wouldn't hold. She could only see him lost.

I smell Mira again, strong and red. She is in the distance with the boy. She is the cluster of thoughts Brother seeks while I desire the whole sky, death, the boy, a living map, a butcher's chart.

They're looking across a slight depression criss-crossed by the shatter lines of cracked mud round black water, to my nose salty but drinkable. They splash in the pool and fill their containers. Death will not hurt but the boy can't hear me. Animals are frightened away by the smell of my dry mouth. There are ruins where a dune sea meets the grey-and-black rock plain and the air smells of cinnamon. Our kingdom. I will bring Brother to these chambers. Sand and wind have removed every roof and rounded every edge yet under the sand between walls are tile floors, vermilion, azure, gold, and the place is haunted not only by the souls of hunters and kings but by a million killed creatures: lion, tiger, antelope, gazelle, a dense blue aftermath of ancient animals. Cousin predators crouch round a gold table and other tethered beasts with heavy plates and spikes and plumes sprawl in the shadows while their owners tell stories of past kills. How they never encountered a species without taming one of its kind.

It's beautiful, Mira says.

I hide behind a wall and listen to the boy's breath, this boy's life, the taste of that, that he has not yet killed. But the dog finds me first.

At first Sapporo and the photographer skirt the sand, stay on the plain, but then they have to cross a tongue of dunes. She takes pictures of him stumbling. He tells her he lost grandparents, mother, father, wife, son, everyone. He tells her he lost everyone. *Liar.* He held a baton between his fingers, stood in front of an orchestra in Sapporo, a city on the island of Hokkaido designed by Americans and built on the ruins of a settlement of the old ones. He was born in the middle of that city, on the rubble of a conquered people. A tribe of ghosts. His ancestral home was a small island off the southwest coast of Hokkaido. Everyone lived there, his whole family. The woman laughs at him as he picks himself up again and shakes sand from his hair. "Why did you leave Japan?" she asks.

"To come here," he says.

For a while they're on the flat, then in dunes again. An entire night climbing one yellow hill. Moonlight bright as sun. Every moment a getting up from falling. He's incapable of asking a question. They observe the horizon, study the ground. Their feet kick stones. They see two travellers a long way off, lose them behind a dune.

The boy crouches and his little penis spurts, sand droplets roll downhill, turds collapse into the scooped hole and he looks up at the woman and tells her a beetle will lay eggs on his shit. Ah, the moon freezes their shadows, such a way she touches the skin at the small of his back. Then the sun flattens them and wind piles sand between them and they rest in the shade of the blanket draped across two sticks. She lies back and opens her mouth for the boy to drip water into her mouth. I open my mouth to the black specks of birds circling above.

I'm tough-skinned, loose-limbed, blood-warm after the moon has risen. I love the way Brother rolls grains between his fingers, but the photographer sees me and waves at the grey plain and, Look! she calls. I've found her, found Mira, I want to tell him, she's with a boy, they're on the move, I want to cut him from the pack and eat him up, Mira too, her slowness gives me the right. Brother's eyes warn me off, my ugly shadow.

I'm close to a kill when the boy's stride grows wider and they hit the roadbed and soon it's cigarette butts and crushed beer cans, things of the world. Fenced compound, small dwellings, belt of palm trees. The dog has learned to bark at danger. The boy raises his eyebrows at Mira then switches the donkey's rump and the donkey kicks dust. My last chance to extend claws and touch her neck, but her thoughts take shelter in the city again and the moments shear off. Ghost rain evaporates above the ground and veiled women in white headdresses surround me and the dog runs toward the huts.

Slowly Mira and Daam made their way toward the largest of the round buildings. Faint stars above, after the rain. A fire and a griddle. Women and children barefoot in the dust. In the twilight a little girl came forward and patted the donkey's neck. The donkey followed her down a steaming lane past sleeping chickens ranged along a low wall. From the lane came Sapporo and a Japanese woman.

"What a world that has such people in it!" Mira said.

The boy tapped his stick at the hard ground in front of her feet. "Canada," he said. "Tell him."

Sapporo and the boy slept with the men in one house, Mira and the photographer with the women in another.

Veiled women cooked breakfast in the little courtyard, then sang prayers. The dog and the boy waited outside the women's door, eating flatbread and curds and beans. Sapporo stood by the fire looking at the desert. Mira stepped from the women's hut into the light. The boy could not take his eyes off her. The dog would not leave the boy's side. The women sewed together fragments of cloth. Mira and the photographer sat on an old carpet in the shade between the two buildings. Beyond the courtyard men smoked and laughed till the sky was white-hot.

Next day the same. The women's quick flying fingers. The long hot noon. The boy came from the men's hut with his belongings wrapped in a bundle. Mira and the photographer made room for him between them. The dog flopped down, nose on paws, sighing.

The women wake me they roll me onto my side they slip hands under my legs and arms and lift me high, He will not need you now, he will not need you again, no more rivers, no more oceans, no more islands, no exile, no home. Hush, you're the last one, Kagura. Hush, you are the last. Hush.

I quit in the middle of the night the ocean of sleepers round me and crawl to the boy. We sit on the gravel and wait for my head to spill highways and continents. I tell him it's all right to be last because loneliness will fade, this old commonwealth will not endure. O heart, O blood, O breath. Let's bark at the sky and sink into wildness.

Brother and I in the sun don't know what to do. A white pigeon lands. We've never said this goodbye before.

Sapporo touched the top of the boy's head. "We are going home." He laughed at Mira. "Where did you find that funny dog?" He put an arm around her. "I keep remembering my son."

"I'm sorry I never met him," she said.

The rubble underfoot was grey and black. From here everything wavered: Sapporo and Mira, the flaming sky, the dog waltzing in their wake. Sun ablaze in the boy's eyes. The Japanese photographer kneeling to aim her camera at them, at the village, then turning.

The city was large on the horizon. A small bird flew straight up and plummeted, wings folded, back to earth, then repeated the flight again and again. The air twanged. The sun came up and silver droplets shook from the bird.

I am hurt through nostrils through wobbly air past Brother and his wife to the boy's delicious skin but not to name it or the stray hairs on his neck or the curve of his back the bones like knuckles.

ELEVEN

Sacred Trees

Men in uniform were pulling charred bodies out of
smouldering huts and setting them side by side while women
with kerchiefs over their mouths collected and tagged the
limbs of children. The living raised flasks to drink water
and avoid one another's eyes and struggled in silence
while vultures hopped and flapped in the burnt grass.
The air smelled of gasoline and meat. News teams arrived
in minibuses and correspondents walked around crying
then sat in their vehicles and made phone calls and keyed
in stories. The boy held the dog by the scruff of her neck.
There were three trees in this village: one already gaunt and
cinder-black, one with small flames licking along branches
on one side and green leaves fluttering on the other, and the
third as yet whole and full of noisy birds.

Each bristles with huge splintered branches. Thick
roots curve into yellow ground. The city looms close and

jets stream overhead. The boy sits in the shade cradling his gun, the earth around him polished by generations of feet. He is a raw new entity, just this moment lodged here.

Smoke winds through the bright leaves. An Australian cameraman with a flask tells her that botanists come from all over the world to study these cypresses. They're four thousand years old. He begins to stutter. Before dawn maybe fifty men ran through the village when most of the people were still asleep and fired into the huts and threw grenades and slashed with machetes those who came out or beat them with clubs and shot the women and children first then the men and poured gasoline on the bodies some still alive and torched them.

Feathers fly from a tattered pair of vultures a soldier has just machine-gunned.

"This is bullshit," said the Australian. "This is out of control."

Mira folds her arms, holds on tight.

"Ah, yeah," said the Australian. He was drunk. She was getting there. "I tell you what. There's a guy over there," he said. "Bloody pundit. On and on about blood rites. Sat next to him on the bus. Christ almighty. I mean fucking amazing. Are you with them then, the Japanese bloke and the kid?" He lit a cigarette. He was trembling.

She rubbed her eyes. "We're together, yeah."

~

"I remember visiting Grandmother on the island when we were children," said Sapporo. "Every day my brother and I would collect things, pebbles, rolled leaves, bone shards, feathers. We left them with her when Father took us home, and next visit they were always gone."

TWELVE

WE WERE IN CLOUDS, NOTHING ABOVE or below. We were going home. We kept saying it. Then we fell asleep. I last saw Kagura running in the smoke and dust, chasing the minibus from the village, the boy's dog leaping round him.

I am a musician. My master died when I was eight. I studied composition in Tokyo and Paris. I led the Sapporo Symphony for a season, then was invited to conduct the Victoria Symphony where my first wife died. My ancestor's ghosts helped me to vanish.

Mira returned to her job and Daam and I stayed in the house. We watched baseball on TV. She came home in the afternoon and I cooked our food. Daam's papers came through. What I most want to say is how rich my life has been. Everything threatened to break my heart, but my heart grew full. We are not allowed to keep chickens in the suburbs, but I keep chickens anyway. Heart remakes itself out of our control. Happiness is a brilliant house tumbling though the dark.

In the winter of Daam's disappearance snow fell on the trees and the sky cleared and the temperature dropped and everything froze so that each time we looked out of the window the view was the same: same snow on each branch, same unchanging scene, no wind to disturb a flake, no flakes to disturb, just blue air that smelled of nothing. Car tires froze. Shoes glued themselves to the ground if you stood still. We wore layers of clothes and searched the streets and heard rumours of sightings and of the exploits of his gang. Once we saw a pack of kids flapping across one of the bridges, but when we got there no one was around. In the spring, we often saw him among a group of children, but the closer we got the faster they spun away, leaving a shiny afterglow in the dusk streets. Summer flew by and the following winter was even harder and colder than the last but Daam came home. He was sick and strung out, no longer a boy, but a thin and haunted young man, and it was simple, what he had to say. "We tell stories. We sleep where we want. We don't need anyone."

Most mornings we collected and cleaned the eggs, fed and watered the chickens, then walked to the baseball diamond and took turns at bat. His arms grew strong and the scars faded. His shaking stopped. He would say nothing about his friends. We sat at the piano and struck the keys. Our butts scrunched on the stool. The dogs barking. Leaves and birds burning. Daam was twenty-six. It seems important now.

If I unlock the rhythm of those days, look back and give my body a shake, everything seems all right. What I'm doing now in this cold cellar seems all right. Writing this down. The shadows, the water dripping from the ceiling, the people and animals who pass through. I'm tired. Here's a single rooster feather recently dropped, still bright with oil. What to make of the sound of it against my beard, the feel of the quill in my mouth? Kagura and I once lay in the dark and masturbated each other while in the next room Grandmother snored like a wolf. At the soup kitchen last week a woman asked me how I liked my new teeth, how they fit, and I said good, and she cheered.

THIRTEEN

Kagura

I recognised him right away in the opening of an alley behind some shops, just at that time when the light goes grey. He stopped at a smell then turned quickly, nostrils twitching. He caught my movement and his heels thudded against the sidewalk as he tried to get away. My touch calmed him but he didn't know me. His eyes were wide and bright as ever, but how old and bent he was now, unable to raise his face to the sky.

We roamed and lay down under the stars, a different place each night, the bond between us all my making. When he slept I slept. When he struggled to his feet to piss, I pissed beside him. Getting food occupied both of us. He was warm and angular, soft in the middle, full of groans and laments, his old fierceness gone. Not quite. Still old doubts. Small terrors.

I never return to the house where I lived with Mira and Daam. I was not good at women. We have our winter squat where we lie together at night on newspaper and rags beneath the church, and in the morning feed the chickens, break the ice on their water, collect their eggs.

Who knows how long since a congregation gathered above to sing and pray? Who knows how long it will be before the roof falls down on our heads? The bell tower timbers are black from an old fire. The foundations are crumbling, the walls are sinking. Splintered boards across the doors and windows green with moss. This place used to be a marsh and in spring, soon now, the river will overflow and sewers back up and the cellar will fill with bloated earthworms. We will have to move. Moulds already colour the floor. I have found purple robes, old books, statues, portraits, everything soaked and dried many times, transformed by fungi and the gnawing of rats. My hands are always cold. When it rains the chickens in the graveyard trees are sodden.

Kagura is frail. He almost falls when he shakes himself. When we were boys I loved a pot-bellied toy gorilla. He loved a beautiful doll, a princess. We sat on the floor, our spines as straight as we could make them, and played with our toys. I felt ashamed of my gorilla and envied him the princess.

The moment the car hits Kagura I am screaming. A crowd of pedestrians waits for a green light. He glances off the vehicle. A man's blurred face swivels behind glass. The car doesn't even slow down. Kagura staggers and sprawls in the traffic, but no one moves, no one steps out to help. Then he's up and running and I'm after him on a last journey, a turmoil of breath and spray and blood. Nothing else. Two chasing creatures. Nothing else. When I catch him he stands trembling and we are interested in something we have always known but are learning to apply for the first time, in spite of his pain and my helplessness. We are caught by what we dimly know. He whimpers. I stroke his body. He turns and sniffs at a scent I can't single out. The buildings lean. People are stopping in the street. The rain beats down. I wipe my tears on the fur of his cheek. A drop of blood quivers on one nostril. It's all right, Kagura, it's only me. But a doll knows a child better than Kagura knows me. A child knows the warrior's spin. The child's arms reaching again. It's all right. I'll stay with you. Pedestrians edge round us. No one knows who we are. Kagura gets down on the pavement. Licks his lips. His shoulders and legs begin to convulse. He makes a puddle of piss. I carry him home to the church on my back, his heart faint through the numbness of my shoulder. He won't take food, won't drink, won't open his eyes. The child had a rosy cheek. The monster had a hard life. His body has no weight at all.

The church buildings are sinking into rising water. My hands are frozen. Every week it's harder to climb down to my place, to navigate the broken steps. The blackened timbers groan. Small creatures live here in the dark, under the water, emerging at night to feed. Frogs sing. From time to time, now that it's spring, children with flashlights play down here on a raft, terrifying one another and mad with laughter. I curl round him and try to sleep. He's getting ready to die. His breathing, heavy with mucous, rattles in his throat.

Once he was a young monster who hated and adored me. We walked to school past North Gate Shrine, through the old temple courtyard. He held my hand across a foggy field. There were unfinished houses, and after school we played in half-framed rooms. Summers our father took us to Grandmother's island where we ran wild. He was a thing to know, a thing to love. A thing I didn't know I had. I stroke his hair and his eyes open slightly. Every breath a shudder. The chickens have abandoned the churchyard. I must find a dry cave where we can live. I must build a shrine. Everything spoils in this cellar. I don't know where they've settled, my eight hens and my rooster. It's terribly cold. I must find some old wood and build a shelter.

I know before my eyes are open. Puddles in the empty church reflect back my pale face. Nothing to mourn, nothing to bury.

I'm going to look for eggs — there must be some the children have not trampled, some still whole among the graves.

Here comes a brand new thought all ready to polish: what I felt in my life, all my life, what I called loneliness, was nothing but smoke and oil. I regret nothing. I am tranquil. I'll begin tomorrow. It doesn't matter whether or not I finish.

FOURTEEN

ALL CHILDREN RISE UP IN THE end and sink in the beginning, already lost, every child. Look at them. Every son and daughter opens and closes between one step and the next. I hold my breath. I love them yet can never get close.

The time we have together amounts to smoke and oil. We give up to each other forgotten parts of ourselves. We are beautiful. The dead are not lost. I love my parents, love them still, and I love birds, all birds. Writing makes us intimate with loss, and if we give in to it, we come upon ourself. So this is for you and for my ancestors. This is for the children.

Michael Kenyon was born in Sale, England, and has lived on the West Coast since 1967. His work has been shortlisted for the Commonwealth Writers Prize, the SmithBooks/Books in Canada First Novel Award, the Baxter Hathaway Prize in fiction, *The Malahat Review* Novella Prize, *Prism international*'s fiction contest, the Journey Prize, the National and the *Western Magazine* Award. He has worked as a seaman, a diver and a taxidriver. Now he divides his week between Pender Island and Vancouver, having in both places a private therapeutic practice.